D0442821

# SWITCHED

## ALSO BY BRUCE HALE

**Class Pets**

#1: *Fuzzy's Great Escape*

#2: *Fuzzy Takes Charge*

#3: *Fuzzy Freaks Out*

#4: *Fuzzy Fights Back*

*Big Bad Detective Agency*

# SWITCHED

Bruce Hale

SCHOLASTIC PRESS | NEW YORK

Library of Congress Cataloging-in-Publication Data available

ISBN 978-1-338-64591-0

10 9 8 7 6 5 4 3 2 1 21 22 23 24 25

Printed in Italy 183

First edition, April 2021

Book design by Keirsten Geise

To Riley for inspiration,
and to Jose for heart

# CONTENTS

# PARKER ⇨

## 1

# Powder-Blue Rabies

It had taken all afternoon to set up, but it only took five minutes for the dog to destroy everything.

As soon as everyone else had left the house on errands, Parker Pitts had hustled like mad, trying to make everything perfect for the farewell party for his big sister, Billie. He'd vacuumed, tidied, and dusted the whole downstairs (much more thoroughly than Mom ever had). He'd festooned the dining room with blue streamers, party hats, and musical notes cut from shiny golden paper.

Heck, he'd even gotten their neighbor Mrs. Johnson to drive him to pick up the cake from the bakery. It was powder blue (Billie's favorite color), decorated with musical notations and an edible microphone on top (all his idea).

The cake sat on the table. His mom would pick up the Thai takeout on her way home.

All was perfect—just the way Parker liked things to be.

Restless, he readjusted the place settings he'd made from

Dad's scratched vinyl records and repositioned the bass clef centerpiece just so. He was ready. Everything was set to make Billie's send-off for her semester abroad a truly magical experience.

As six o'clock struck, his mom's and dad's cars pulled into the driveway almost simultaneously. That alone made it a red-letter day. Parker couldn't remember the last time they'd both been home for dinner together.

Gee, and all it took to make this rare event happen was one of their kids leaving town.

At the *thunk-thunk* of car doors and the happy chatter of everyone coming up the walkway, Parker smiled. He loved how his family was a rainbow of color, from his mahogany-skinned dad to his wheat-skinned mom, with he and Billie falling somewhere in between. His grandma used to be on the walnut-colored end of that spectrum, but—

With an effort, he forced away the thought of her. What you didn't think about couldn't hurt you.

The front door swung open. "We're home!" his mom called.

Right away, the *clickety-clack* of doggie toenails scrabbled on the entryway's wooden floor. Thunderous footfalls and thuds from bumped furniture marked the progress of Boof, Billie's shaggy goldendoodle.

Parker gritted his teeth.

*That dog.*

He burst into the dining room like a dirty-blond hurricane. Making straight for Parker, the dog reared up on his hind legs, planted two massive paws on Parker's chest, and bathed his face with a tongue funkier than fifty weeks' worth of dirty gym socks.

Parker staggered back.

"Yuck!" Twisting away from the creature, he swabbed at his slimy face with a forearm. Now he'd have to go wash again. "Bad dog! Down!"

Nothing he said seemed to sink in. Of course, that wasn't surprising, given that Boof had flunked out of the Perfect Puppy Academy and that Billie rarely bothered to reinforce the few commands the dog did learn.

Boof jumped up again. This time, one of his sharp toenails caught on Parker's shirt pocket. When Parker tried to shove the dog away, the fabric tore with a loud *r-r-r-rip.*

His favorite *Star Wars* T-shirt, wrecked.

Parker's face flushed hot. "Bills!" he cried. "Get this thing away from me!"

Bored of jumping, Boof thrust his nose into Parker's crotch and took a loud, deep whiff. Parker raised a knee, spinning away.

"Billie!"

Gliding into the room like a long-necked princess in ripped jeans and an explosion of curls, Billie patted her thighs. "Come here, Boofie-Boof. Is the widdle puppy bugging my widdle brudder? Is he?"

The mop-haired dog thwacked his tail back and forth, knocking paper party hats off the chair and onto the floor. Amber eyes shining, he padded over to Billie and licked her face up one side and down the other.

Parker shuddered. "*Little* puppy? He weighs almost as much as I do." He collected the hats, wondering if they'd been contaminated by dog germs. Could you sterilize paper hats?

Just then, Billie noticed the decorations. Her mouth fell open in an O, and her hazel eyes widened. "For me?"

Parker nodded.

"Oh, P-man, you're the best!" She beamed so broadly her eyes disappeared into slits. Rushing forward, Billie gave him a fierce hug. "I'm going to miss you, bro."

"Yeah, I know," said Parker, ducking his head.

His throat tightened. Though she was four years older and technically his half sister, that didn't matter. Ever since Grandma Mimi had helped them bridge their differences five years ago, Parker and Billie had been pretty tight. He was really going to miss her.

Of course, if he admitted this to Billie, her head would swell so big she'd never fit through the airplane door. So he let her guess.

"Ooh, and that cake!" she squealed, squeezing her hands together. "Total coolness!"

Parker couldn't hide his grin. "Thought you'd like it," he mumbled. Then his skin prickled with drying dog slobber and he shivered. "Um, be right back."

Parker hurried into the kitchen and blasted the hot water, vigorously scrubbing his face and hands with soap. Too bad Boof wasn't like the animals from some of his favorite fantasy tales, all helpful and full of natural wisdom. He was no Aslan of Narnia. In fact, as far as Parker could tell, this dog's wisdom consisted primarily of knowing which cat poop was the crunchiest.

"Did you tidy up around here again?" asked his mom, setting some takeout bags on the counter. She squeezed his shoulders and smooched the back of his head as he washed. As you'd expect of the city's top Realtor, she was impeccably turned out, today in a copper-colored dress that matched the highlights in her hair. "You really didn't have to."

Parker shrugged. "I wanted to." Drying his face with a fresh dish towel, he reflected that it felt more like he *had* to. Ever since Mimi . . . well, ever since then, he *really* wanted to keep things at home clean and well ordered. It made him feel better. And like Mimi always used to say, a tidy room makes for a tidy mind.

At the thought of his grandma, Parker's lips clamped tight and his chest felt heavier than a mountain of regrets.

She should've been here tonight. His Mimi *loved* a party.

In that moment, Parker missed her like a beached whale misses the waves. He sucked in a ragged breath, casting around for something else to clean.

Just then, his dad sauntered into the kitchen. As usual, his tie was askew, his cobalt shirt looked like it had never met an iron, and his tweed jacket was rumpled. The overall effect was like an unmade bed with a potbelly.

"What's the word, Bird?" he asked. "Good day today?"

"Not bad." Parker sponged up the spilled water around the sink, hiding a shy smile. He loved when his dad called him Bird, the nickname of Charlie Parker, an old-timey sax player he was named after. In fact, his dad was such a jazz fan, he and his first wife had named Billie after some long-ago singer. Between Dad's music professor job and Billie's talents, it was a tuneful household, to say the least.

"Mmm, that smells good." Parker's dad rummaged in one of the takeout bags, cracking open a cardboard container and lifting out some flat noodles. "Pad Thai with chicken?" He slurped down the noodles and went back for more.

"And spring rolls, *and* shrimp curry, *and* garlic eggplant," said his mom. She hip-checked her husband, swatting his hand away from the food. "All her favorites."

Belatedly, Parker detected the rich aromas of Thai food—lemongrass, garlic, fish sauce. Somehow, he was always the last to notice smells.

"Wow, you guys did all this for me?" Billie stood in the doorway, a mile-wide smile splitting her face. "I didn't expect a party."

"It's not every day my little girl goes off to a fancy Irish performing arts school," said Parker's dad.

"Dad, I'm not a—" Billie began.

But whatever she'd intended to say was drowned out by a tremendous crash from the dining room behind her.

"What was that?" asked Parker.

Billie spun around. "Boof!"

Rushing to the doorway and peering past his sister's shoulder, Parker witnessed a sight that turned his blood colder than a holiday on the ice planet Hoth. His breath died in his throat. Somehow, Boof had clambered up onto the table, destroying the centerpiece and scattering the place settings. Legs braced wide, he was gobbling up Billie's cake with doggie glee.

*"No!"* cried Parker.

"Bad dog!" yelled Billie. They rushed into the room.

Boof's head flew up. His eyes were wild, and his muzzle was thick with frosting, making it look like he had a case of powder-blue rabies. A crepe paper streamer dangled from his neck like a feather boa. Eyeing the humans charging toward him, the dog seemed to think it was all some kind of glorious game.

He gave a puppy bow, chest low, tail wagging.

Then, with a loud *wurf*, he bounded off the table and tore from the room. Billie gave chase. Parker froze, astonishment rooting him in place. He gaped at the wreckage. The bass clef centerpiece was bent in half, two of the vinyl records had shattered, and the cake! The cake was a blue-and-yellow ruin, punctuated with paw prints. As he watched, a clump of frosting dropped off the edge of the table and landed on the floor with a *plop*.

Parker's fists balled. His jaw clenched. His skin itched all over with the burning need to clean up this awful mess right now—right after he strangled that rotten dog.

Then, from the corner of his eye, a flash of violet light caught his attention. Parker did a double take. It looked almost like one of the items on the hutch—a carving of the Yoruba trickster god Eshu that Mimi had given him—was glowing.

A wave of gooseflesh rippled across his shoulders. "No way," he muttered, squeezing his eyes shut. This kind of thing only happened in the movies. Sure enough, when he looked again, the glow had gone. *Just a trick of the light.*

"Oh, honey." His mom came up behind him and rested a hand on his shoulder. "It's okay. Really, it is."

Parker was too busy grappling with his warring impulses (clean or kill?) to look up at her. But he knew she'd be wearing that worried expression she often displayed whenever he got into cleaning mode.

"*Ugh*, that knuckleheaded dog." His dad joined them. "For a while there, I thought he was learning, but I swear he's getting worse."

"Dogs can sense big changes," said his mom. "Maybe this is just normal acting out."

"Normal acting out?" said Parker, picking up a fallen streamer. "Yeah, right. Because normal dogs wreck parties. Normal dogs climb onto tables and eat cakes."

His mom sent him a tight-lipped look, like she disapproved of his sarcasm but was cutting him some slack.

Dad shook his head ruefully. "I told Tina it was a bad idea to give Billie a dog, especially with her semester abroad coming up so soon."

"And since when has your fancy-pants ex ever listened

to you?" The edge in Parker's mom's voice was sharp enough to slice stale bread.

"Tina loves to spoil her—when she happens to remember that Billie exists."

Parker's sister poked her head through the doorway. "Where's Boof?"

"You lost him?" asked Mom.

"He can't have gone far." Parker's dad planted his hands on his hips, scanning the area.

From the kitchen came the rustle of a plastic bag and some serious crunching noises. All four heads turned.

"The food!" yelled Parker.

Feet unfrozen, he hurtled past his parents, back into the kitchen. What he saw sent a hot shot of adrenaline blasting through his body. Boof's paws rested on the counter, and the handles of a plastic takeout bag were disappearing down his gullet like a hobbit into his hole.

"No-no-no!" Parker charged forward. He snatched at the bag but missed when Boof lunged away and galloped past.

With a wordless cry, Parker dashed after him.

From behind came his dad's shout: "*What?!* Not the pad Thai!"

Parker's eyes narrowed. Two impulses wrestled inside him: He burned to get his hands on that mutt, and he yearned to clean up the mess the dog had left. For now, stopping the doggie demolition derby came first.

Down the hallway he pounded, chasing the blond blur of Boof.

The dog glanced back with one wild, white-rimmed eye.

He was *enjoying* this.

And then they rounded the corner, and Billie stepped out, arms spread wide. "Gotcha!" The dog's paws skidded. Before Boof could slip away, she snagged his collar, yanking him to a halt. "Bad Boofie!"

As Parker caught up, he witnessed the last of the bag disappearing into the dog's mouth. "Your 'Boofie' ate our dinner," he said.

"Oh, no." Taking the beast's shaggy head between her hands, Billie bent down to look into his amber eyes. "All of it?"

"The noodles."

"Yikes."

"He swallowed the bag whole," said Parker. "And most of the container."

Billie's face blanched. "Call the vet! We've got to get it out of him. He might die."

Boof's tail thumped against the floor. He licked her face with what looked like yards of tongue.

"Yeah, seems like he's sinking fast," said Parker.

Together, they closed the dog in his crate so he couldn't destroy anything else. After some initial whining, Boof turned around three times, flopped down with a grunt, and began gently gnawing on his bedding.

Dad phoned the vet.

Collapsing onto a kitchen chair, Parker stared at the floor. His heart thudded dully in his chest.

"Ruined," he said. "All ruined."

Billie squatted beside him, rubbing his back in gentle circles. "Come on, P-man, we've still got the rest of the Thai food. And I bet we could salvage some cake."

Parker couldn't meet her gaze. "It's a puppy apocalypse." He quivered at the thought of the mess. It made him itch like foxtails under the skin. *Not another second.* Parker surged to his feet and fetched a fresh sponge, a roll of paper towels, some kitchen gloves, and a garbage bag. With a heavy sigh, he set to work cleaning up.

⇦BOOF

# 2

# Possum Belly

Boof didn't get it. Good-smelling things should feel good inside you.

So how could something that smelled as amazing as the family's meal feel so funny in his gut? Even cat poop wasn't this rough going down. Mysterious things rumbled and bubbled and burbled inside as he lay there chewing his bedding.

But that wasn't the worst of it.

Boof was all alone, and his family didn't love him anymore.

He whined again. The humans in the other room ignored him. His Sweet Girl had shouted at him, which she almost never did. Boof curled his tail under at the thought. He'd never felt this bad before. Probably.

Why was everyone so mad? He'd smelled the anger rolling off them in waves, along with Gloomy Boy's usual scent of sadness. All Boof wanted was for everyone to love him. He *was* lovable, right?

What was wrong? Why didn't anyone want to play?

They were all in the other room now, eating their meal, talking their human talk. Without him. Boof's place was beside the table, with his Sweet Girl slipping him scraps when nobody was looking. He belonged with his family.

Boof heaved a heavy sigh. Hanging out in his little cave was all well and good when he could come and go as he pleased, but to be shut in here like a barely weaned puppy?

So unfair.

Why couldn't he be with his Sweet Girl and have everyone be happy, calling him "good dog" and petting him? Was that too much to ask? True, Gloomy Boy had been sad ever since Boof had known him—suffering cats, he didn't even respond to doggie kisses! But the rest of the family had been mostly happy. Not anymore. For days now, they'd been running around acting excited, but being all tense and bothered underneath.

Something was up, and it made him anxious.

Usually eating, chewing, and running around helped calm him down. But not today. Boof stood up, turned about several times, lay down, and sighed again.

After what felt like forever, Gloomy Boy and his mother,

Flower Woman, carried dishes into the room. They scraped the extra food down some magical hole where it disappeared (*What a waste—I'll eat it!*) and washed and dried the plates.

Every time Gloomy Boy shot him a dirty look, Boof thumped his tail hopefully. *Who can even remember what all the fuss was about? We're friends, right?*

But each time, the Boy turned away scowling.

After Flower Woman had gone, Gloomy Boy spent a long time sprinkling powder on the counter and floor, and rubbing them. His energy was edgy, spiky. Time and time again, Boof showed him the big puppy eyes, signaling that it was okay to pet him. But the Boy paid no attention.

After he left, nobody came by in, like, *forever.* Boof stewed in his loneliness. At long last, Sweet Girl's dad, Ball Man, strode in and squatted down before the cave door.

"You feeling okay?" he asked. "The vet said to keep an eye on you."

Although he recognized *vet* (not one of his favorite human words), Boof responded to the gentle tone with a warm look.

"You going to be a good dog now?"

Thumping his tail, Boof licked the man's hand where it

gripped the bars of the cave. This was more like it. Wasn't he always a Good Dog?

"All right, come on, then." Ball Man opened the door.

Boof didn't need to be asked twice. He emerged from the cave, stretched, and shook himself vigorously. Then he wound around the man's legs, wagging with all his might and soaking up lots of good petting.

*Yay, he was a Good Dog again!*

Ball Man wandered off without throwing the ball for him. Probably an oversight. Thirsty from his strange dinner, Boof slurped up half the water from his bowl by the door. Then he trotted off to find Sweet Girl.

She was upstairs in her room, sitting on her bed, folding socks. Beside her, a big boxlike thing full of clothes lay spread across the bed. A sad, worried scent wafted off the Girl, and the corners of her mouth pulled downward.

Boof nudged her leg, then rested his chin on her thigh.

Petting the top of his head, Sweet Girl let her hand drift down to scratch behind the ears in his favorite place.

*Oh, yeah. That's it.*

"Feeling better?" she asked.

He gave an extra-strength wag.

"There's my good boy," she said. "There's my Boofie-woofie." And her voice was so sad he wanted to howl like a lonesome wolf. Instead, he leaned into her.

"Oh, Boofie. I'm going to miss you something fierce." The Girl's voice wobbled. She touched her forehead to the top of his head and caressed his ears the way he liked.

Boof felt confused. Usually getting petted was a happy thing for everyone. What was happening here?

Straightening, she looked down at him. "I know this is a big opportunity. Everyone says I should be excited about it, and I am. But . . ."

Gazing at her, Boof soaked up the attention. This was the most time she'd spent with him in days and days. She hadn't walked him, hadn't talked to him, and had spent way too much time away from the house doing who knew what.

Holy gopher guts, it was enough to make a lesser dog feel antsy and unwanted.

But this? This was more like it.

"I've never been away from home before," Sweet Girl continued. "You know? I mean, what if I get homesick? What if nobody likes me? What if everyone else is more talented than me?"

Boof didn't know what she was talking about. But he knew when one of his humans needed some love. His snout burrowed under her arm, pushing up against her side until a broken chuckle escaped the Girl's lips.

"Oh, Boofie. You always know how to cheer me up. I can't believe I'll be away from you for three whole months. What will I do without my puppy?" Taking an ear in each hand, she waggled Boof's head back and forth.

He didn't understand much human talk, but he could read her happy-sad tone as clearly as a squirrel's scent trail. Something was definitely up with his Sweet Girl.

When *he* was troubled, a walk usually helped. Boof nudged her leg, then took a few steps toward the bedroom doorway, dropping her a hint.

She didn't get it (humans could be so slow), so he repeated the action, adding the big eyes this time. Sweet Girl frowned.

"Sorry, puppy. No time for walkies. I've got to pack all my toiletries, decide which clothes to take—"

"Hey, Bills." Gloomy Boy leaned in through the doorway. He spotted Boof and glared. "What's *he* doing out?"

Retreating to his Girl's side, Boof looked up at him with total innocence. Honestly, he had no idea why the Boy was mad at him. Boof was the most lovable dog around, after all.

Sweet Girl scruffled the fur on his back. "Aw, Boofie didn't mean anything by it," she said. "He's just being Boof, that's all."

"Really?" Gloomy Boy cocked his head. "So, no big deal, Attila the Hun was just being Attila the Hun?"

She chuckled. "Boof as a barbarian invader? I don't quite see it."

"This rotten dog wrecks your farewell party and all is forgiven?" The Boy's fists planted on his hips, and his anger smell sharpened.

"Lighten up, bro," said the Girl. "Seriously. So he made a mess. It's not that big a deal."

Gloomy Boy rolled his eyes. "Not a big deal? Someone always has to clean up his messes, you know."

Offering up a tight smile, Sweet Girl said, "Did you need something? I'm trying to finish packing."

That sad smell rolled off Gloomy Boy again, like the whiff of a dead fish by the lakeshore. "Nah. I just wanted to say 'safe trip.'"

"Aww."

He bit his lip. "I wish . . . I wish Mimi could've been here to see you. She would've been so proud." When Gloomy Boy's voice warbled, Boof padded over to lean on his leg and offer some comfort. The Boy didn't pet him, but he didn't push him away either.

"I know," said Sweet Girl. "And we probably wouldn't be talking like this now if it wasn't for her."

"Definitely," said the Boy.

Sweet Girl looked down at the socks in her lap. Now *she* was the one sending out sadness vibes. Boof re-joined her.

"Bummer that you won't be around for my birthday," said the Boy.

She glanced up. "You trying to make me feel guilty?"

"No," said Gloomy Boy. "It's only—I'm really going to m—"

Just then, her little talking box played a melody, and Sweet Girl held it to her ear. "Rashida?" She shrugged at the Boy, pointing to her device. When he slouched out of the room, she collapsed back onto the bed. "Oh, I know. I'm going to miss you too. What? No, I'm still packing . . ."

Twice more, Boof bumped her, trying to encourage a walk, but his Girl kept shoving his head away. Finally, she shooed him out the door, talking all the while, and closed it behind her.

Why couldn't she just spend time with him? What was wrong? Did she not love him anymore? Anxious energy bubbled inside him.

Boof pawed at the door. He *wurf*ed softly. When this got no response, he gave in to his thirst, trotting down to that room with the huge water bowl.

The urine smells were strong here, and Boof took a deep whiff to savor them before settling in to lap up the water. Suffering cats, he was thirsty—couldn't seem to get enough to drink. And it felt like a bad-tempered possum was burrowing through his belly.

Boof looked around. What he needed was somewhere to put his energy. As a test, he pawed the white paper roll beside the bowl. It unwound, leaving a pleasing trail. He pawed it again, and more paper unspooled.

Inspired, Boof seized the roll in his mouth—it came out pretty easily—and carried it into the hallway for chewing. This wasn't as satisfying as he'd hoped (the paper was soft and flavorless), so he batted at the roll. It bounced down the hall.

Now, this was more like it!

Boof gave chase, keeping the cylinder moving with his nose and paws, until finally it got away from him and—*bip-bip-bip*—went bounding down the stairs. He barked, watching it bounce step by step. At last, it reached the flat place and fetched up against Gloomy Boy's shoes.

"Dad!" Anger smells radiated from the Boy like stink from a skunk. "Boof's making a mess again!"

A bedroom door opened. When Ball Man saw Boof's experiment, he didn't make the play gesture. Instead, he crossed his arms.

"Someone needs another time-out. Back in the crate for you, doggo." Snagging Boof's collar with one hand, he led him downstairs. Gloomy Boy began gathering up the paper, and as Boof and the man passed by, he said three words to them:

"Worst. Dog. Ever."

Boof hung his head. Gloomy Boy didn't approve, Ball Man wouldn't play, and Sweet Girl had no time for him. Being a dog was so hard sometimes.

# PARKER ⇨

# 3

# A Trouble Doubleheader

As mind-numbingly awful as the evening had been, Parker didn't think things could get much worse. He was wrong. Sometime after midnight, he was having a vivid dream about a laughing, vital Mimi making dinner for the Yoruba gods. She'd always told him that dreams were a way for those in the spirit world to talk to the living, and Dream Mimi was just about to tell him something important, when a hand rocked his shoulder.

"Honey, get up," his mom commanded.

A sharp sense of loss knifed through Parker. The only way he could see his grandma was in dreams, and now this one had been shattered.

Blinking the stickiness from his eyes, Parker yawned. Sludge oozed through his veins. His limbs felt heavier than a jumbo jet on Jupiter. "Wh-what time is it?"

"I need your help."

Parker rolled over, knocking to the floor the book he'd

fallen asleep reading. "Can't Dad do it?" he mumbled.

His mother shook his shoulder harder. "He took your sister to the airport. He's not back yet."

Foggily, Parker recalled that Billie was catching the early-early morning flight to Ireland. He groaned. Struggling to sit up, he croaked, "What's wrong?"

"Boof's making weird sounds. I'm afraid we might have to take him to an emergency pet hospital."

*That lousy dog. Again.* Parker sighed an epic sigh, swung his legs over the edge of the mattress, and stood up.

His mom was already at the doorway. "Come on, let's go."

When they reached the kitchen, Boof stood in his crate, head hanging low. He stared up at them, saucer-eyed under dirty-blond bangs. Mom wasn't exaggerating. The dog was making a sporadic hiccupping noise like *heeeyurch* and moaning to himself.

*Serves you right*, thought Parker. Then he instantly felt bad for thinking that. As Billie had said, the dog was just being a dog.

Boof's stomach made a peculiar growling noise, like a wolverine caught in a washing machine.

"What do we do?" asked Parker.

"Let's try letting him out first," said his mom. "Maybe he has to poop."

Parker's skin crawled at the thought, but he unlatched the crate and helped his mom herd Boof out the doggie door into the backyard.

The night was chilly, raising gooseflesh on his arms and legs under the thin pajamas. A lopsided moon shone down on the toast-brown autumn lawn and the wooden picnic table with benches, abandoned since the weather changed.

As soon as Boof stepped outside, he beelined it for the back corner of the yard. There, he hunched, teetering forward and back.

"Poor guy doesn't know which end to let it out of," said Parker's mother.

"Mom!"

"Well, it's true."

As Parker watched in horrified fascination, the dog staggered a few steps, hunched again, and with a noise like a dingo's death rattle, horked up his stolen meal in a stream of half-digested food and cardboard fragments.

"Yuck!" Parker covered his eyes, and then found he couldn't help peeking.

Once more, Boof ralphed up the contents of his stomach. How could a dog's belly hold so much?

"That's *so* gross." Parker turned away.

"At least it's coming out," said his mom.

Another moan from the dog, then . . . nothing.

"I think that's it," said Parker's mother.

"Oh, good. I thought he'd spew up the *Titanic* next."

The odor of half-digested Thai food and doggie stomach acid wafted across the yard. Parker gagged. Seeing that disgusting puddle of glop, he was dismayed to feel the same impulse he felt when he witnessed a mess in the kitchen. The prickling sensation started in his palms and began to build. He gritted his teeth, but the feeling spread up his arms and across his shoulders, until . . .

"Aaugh! I can't stand it!" cried Parker.

He hustled into the kitchen and emerged with rubber gloves, a huge wad of paper towels, a garbage bag, and air freshener. Parker spritzed the freshener in a wide swath. And as he bent to mop up the dog's orangey barf, his mom smiled and nodded.

"I think it's great that you're pitching in with the dog," she said.

"Well . . ." Parker couldn't tell her that it wasn't a choice. He just had to do it; that was the way he was.

"And the timing couldn't be better."

"Why's that?" he asked, trying to breathe through his mouth. "Is it National Dog Barf Day?" This stuff really was nasty. Parker dropped some sodden towels into the garbage bag and reached for fresh ones.

Chafing her arms against the cool breeze, his mom said, "You'll have to get used to taking care of him anyway, so you may as well start now."

"Wait, what?"

"Honey, you know your dad and I both work. We can't do everything."

"But—"

"As of today, Boof is your responsibility."

"No, no, no. I couldn't—"

"Until Billie returns, he's your dog."

As this news sank in, Parker let his head flop back and he stared up into the pitiless night sky, silently asking, *Why me?* In that moment, he hated his sister, he hated his parents, and most of all, he hated that wretched, disgusting dog called Boof.

⇧⇩

Bleary-eyed and sleep-deprived from his late-night adventure, Parker staggered through his morning routine like a wounded coyote dragging a spring trap. It wasn't fair, but his dad made him walk Boof before breakfast. And it was drizzling.

Of course.

Parker's nose wrinkled at the funky wet-dog smell.

"Twice a day, little man," said his dad. "Rain or shine.

If he doesn't get exercise, he takes it out on our house."

Parker even had to dish up the disgusting canned dog food, which was so gross he nearly heaved a couple of times before finishing his chore. Probably full of ground-up horse hooves and pig tails.

Or something worse. *Yuck.*

Still, Boof snarfed up the meal with gusto, spraying little bits of dog food everywhere as he gobbled.

Parker's lip curled. He'd have to scour that floor before he left for school or it would bug him all day. Cleaning kept his mind orderly, kept him from thinking about things like Mimi's passing, or how his parents' commutes took them over one of the most dangerous highways in the state, or whether it was likely that Billie's plane would crash into the icy Atlantic, killing everyone in a fiery explosion.

You know, minor stuff like that.

But when Boof bounded into the backyard after eating, and Parker broke out the mop, his mom lifted it from his hands.

"Whoa there, mister. Eat now, tidy up later."

With a jaw-cracking yawn, Parker flopped into his chair and poured himself a bowl of cereal. Without a book to read, he found himself staring blankly at the chair he always avoided—Mimi's vacant seat. Right away,

Parker's thoughts began to run along that dark and well-worn path.

Flinching, he shifted his gaze back to his bowl. Parker didn't know whether it was good that his parents had left the chair there so he wouldn't forget Mimi, or bad because it hurt every time he realized his grandma would never sit there again.

He'd give anything to have her back. And yet, there was nothing he could give, nothing he could do.

These thoughts made him restless. As quickly as possible, Parker slurped up the last of his cereal and gulped down his orange juice, then carried the dirty dishes to the sink to clean them.

His mom looked up from her real estate listings, a spoonful of yogurt halfway to her lips. "Honey, I appreciate the help."

"No problem."

"But you know you don't need to do that."

How could Parker explain? He *did* need to, kind of. It made him . . . calmer, somehow. Even though he knew it wasn't normal for a sixth-grade boy to be so tidy, he really couldn't help himself. He'd always liked being neat. And when Mimi had told him she was the same way and actually encouraged his cleaning up, that sealed the deal.

Of course, the downside was that all that cleaning took

a while. By the time Parker finished washing dishes, he'd missed the bus.

Wonderful.

His mom sighed when he told her. "You were supposed to give us a break from driving you today."

"Sorry, Mom."

"Never mind." She gathered her briefcase from the table. "Get your things together and bring in the dog. I'll drop you on my way to work."

Parker snagged his book bag and jacket. Pushing open the back door, he called, "Boo-oof, come!" and added under his breath, "You rotten mutt."

The goldendoodle pranced inside like Parker had just offered him a roomful of chicken nuggets, his jaws still clamped around a grimy, emerald-green tennis ball. Up he reared, planting two filthy paws on Parker's chest.

"No!" said Parker. "Down!" Twisting, he shoved Boof away. Then he noticed the two muddy smears on his shirt.

"Mom!" He wet a paper towel and dabbed at the mud.

She poked her head through the kitchen doorway, already clad in her nice coat and toting her briefcase and purse.

"You're still here?" she said. "Get in the car, we're late!"

Parker indicated the muddy paw prints. "But my shirt!"

If a day started out with a mess like this, it could easily snowball into something worse. What if the older kids made fun of him? What if he flunked a pop quiz? What if—? "I'll just run upstairs and—"

"No time to change it now," said his mom, glancing at her watch.

"No, but I—"

"Honey, I'll be late for my appointment."

"You don't understand."

His mom scowled. "Parker. Car. Now. You can clean it off as we drive." She popped back out of the room, her heels *click-clacking* down the hallway toward the front door.

Parker glanced down at his shirt and tried to ignore the itchy sensation that bloomed at the sight of it. He narrowed his eyes at the dog. "It's all your fault."

Boof dropped the ball at Parker's feet and looked up, wagging his tail like a furry flag.

"In your dreams." Wheeling about, Parker hurried after his mom, the dog's whine chasing him to the door. Firmly squashing a tiny worm of guilt, he locked up and left the house.

⇧⇩

At school, he hustled through the front gate and into the building, scanning left and right for his buddy Cody. They weren't exactly best friends—Parker's bestie, Miles, had moved away over the summer—but Cody was good enough company. And after all, a guy had to have someone to hang with.

Especially during his first year of middle school.

In the minutes remaining before the first bell, the halls of Wilson P. Wilson Elementary were packed. A babble of voices echoed off the walls, sounding like the bloodthirsty Panem crowd in *The Hunger Games*. As the older kids towered over him, Parker's heart hammered. He wove his way through a group of gabbing seventh-grade girls, past a pair of enormous eighth-grade football players, and over by the wall to watch for his friend.

More than anything, he wished Mimi was still around. She would help him navigate this world in safety. She understood him in a way that his parents never had.

"Parker!" Cody waved, chugging up the hallway. His thick torso was wrapped in a maroon WORLD'S OKAYEST SURFER T-shirt, and his longish blond hair flopped with every step. Then he noticed Parker's chest. "Dude! What happened? Lost a mud-pie-eating contest?"

Parker fished the damp paper towel from his jacket pocket and daubed at the stains again. "Our dumb dog wants to be a clothing designer."

Cody squinted. "Really?"

"Kidding." Sometimes, Parker forgot that his friend was a little slow on the uptake. "Mom and Dad say I have to take care of Boof until Billie gets back."

"Dude, you're majorly lucky," said Cody as they headed for class.

*"Lucky?"*

Cody pushed back his hair. "My parents won't let me have one, and I want a dog brutally bad."

"Really? Take ours," said Parker.

Cody flashed him a sarcastic look. "Ha, ha."

"I'm serious."

"No way your parents would let you give away Billie's dog," said Cody. "And besides . . ."

He said more, but Parker didn't hear it. A vision of loveliness was approaching, and it was as if the whole noisy hallway had gone as silent as a snow-covered slope.

With a toss of her shiny black hair, Gabriella Cortez floated up the corridor beside two of her girlfriends. She laughed at something the redhead said, and Parker couldn't help but notice how utterly even and white her teeth were, like a row of Chiclets. If a more perfect sixth-grade girl existed, he didn't know who that was.

Gabi's posse passed just five feet from Cody and Parker without noticing them. Parker stared. Then, with a burst of giggles and a whiff of some fruity tropical shampoo, the girls glided past and up the hallway.

Cody bumped his arm. "Why didn't you say something?"

"What? To who?"

Rolling his eyes, Cody said, "Duh. Dude, you've got it bad."

"You're dreaming." Parker shifted his grip on his book bag straps, hunched his shoulders, and set off toward their room. "No idea what you're talking about."

"Don't be sham. You always stare at Gabi like she's the last slice of chocolate cake on the plate."

"Do not."

"And whenever she's around, you clam up," said Cody. He jerked his head, flicking the hair from his eyes. "She's never gonna notice you if you don't say something smooth—jeez, anything at all."

Parker scoffed. "Maybe I don't want to bother her." But it sounded weak, even to him.

Cody only snorted.

Pushing past a knot of eighth graders, they rounded the corner and found their path blocked. Deke Wightman stood planted like a redwood tree with a bad attitude, thick arms crossed and a sneer carved on his face. If you looked closely (which nobody wanted to), he had the faintest downy mustache on his upper lip—due, someone said, to the fact that he'd been held back a grade.

Twice.

Deke's piggy little blue eyes lit up when he saw Parker and Cody. As the biggest boy in sixth grade, Deke pretty much had his way with everyone shorter, including over half the seventh-grade class. The best option was to avoid him.

Too late for that. Parker's stomach tightened like a python's coils.

"Hello, hobbits," said Deke. Ever since he'd seen *The Hobbit* movies, that's what he'd been calling everyone shorter than him. Parker didn't bother pointing out that it was more compliment than insult; the hobbit was actually the hero of the story.

"Hey, Deke," he mumbled.

*Avoid eye contact*, he thought. Like pilot fish, Parker and Cody did their best to swim around the shark, but Deke sidestepped into their path.

"Look, I know there's a zero-tolerance bullying policy here," said Deke.

"Uh, yeah," said Cody. He and Parker edged the other way.

Once more, Deke blocked them. "So don't think I'm threatening you."

"Who would ever think that?" said Parker.

"I'm just taking up a collection for a good cause."

"Oh? That's nice." Parker tried cutting back the other way, between the bully and the wall, but Deke closed in, sticking out a grubby palm.

"It's the Deke Memorial Snack Fund. Gimme." The great lump grabbed Parker's shirtfront with his other hand. "Lunch money. Now."

Parker's mouth went as dry as the deserts of Tatooine. He looked to Cody, but his friend had used the opportunity to slip out of reach. Some friend. No teachers roamed the halls; no help was coming.

"I, uh . . ." His shoulders slumped. A bitter taste filled the back of his mouth. It'd be another hungry lunchtime for the Bird. With a faint groan, Parker dug out the two bills and change, handing it over to Deke. "No biggie. I'm on a hunger strike anyway."

Pocketing the money, the bully patted Parker's chest. "Shirt's dirty," he said. "You should fire your maid." And with a laugh that sounded like Chewbacca choking on an ox bone, he lumbered up the hall in search of other prey.

"Thanks for always having my back," said Parker as he and Cody approached their classroom.

"Dude," said his friend. "I know it's totally heinous. But with that monster, it's every man for himself."

What could Parker say? Cody was right. If their roles had been reversed, he'd probably have done the same. The shakedown stank. But, short of waving a bully-banishing magic wand, what could you do about it?

⇧⇩

After that promising start, the day stubbornly refused to get any better. Mrs. Scales assigned extra homework. Parker's math quiz came back with a C-plus. And the role he'd auditioned for in the sixth-grade play went to Vivek Patel. (Gabi, of course, got the female lead. So much for Parker's plan to impress her with his acting.)

Tidying up his desk didn't even go halfway toward calming his mind.

By the time he got home, Parker's mood was darker than a bowl of coal at the bottom of a well on a moonless night. Opening the front door didn't improve it any.

Had it snowed indoors? A sprinkling of white powder covered the entryway floor—powder marked by big, fat paw prints. First, Parker's jaw dropped. Then his book bag.

An enthusiastic *woof!* from deeper in the house greeted him.

Horror-struck, Parker followed the sound down the hall to the family room. The powdery drifts deepened. When he stepped through the doorway, Parker felt like someone had zapped him with a stun gun.

In the middle of the floor lay Boof, tail wagging. His amber eyes peeked out from a mask of pure white, his face and muzzle covered in powder. Between his front legs lay a mostly empty five-pound sack of flour.

Each wag sent a little poof of white dust into the air.

"Boof!" yelled Parker.

The goldendoodle lunged to his feet in a puppy bow. Then, as Parker approached, the dog seized the depleted bag in his jaws and loped away.

"No! Come back here!"

Boof galloped even faster, glancing behind to make sure Parker was chasing.

"Drop it! This isn't a game!"

Around the house they raced, through the kitchen and the dining room, back into the entryway. With each step, the dog left an ever-expanding trail of flour behind him. With each spill, Parker winced.

Finally, on their third go-round, he realized he would never outrun the rotten mutt. Ducking into the kitchen, Parker fished a box of doggie treats from the pantry. At the sound of the cardboard flap opening and waxed paper crinkling, Boof trotted up the hall. He peeked through the doorway.

Parker held out a bone-shaped biscuit. "Come here, you royal pain in the you-know-what."

The dog edged forward, eyes on the treat. When he came within reach, Parker lunged for the flour bag. Boof danced away. Parker growled in frustration, but the golden-doodle just wagged.

"Fine. You want to play a game?" Flinging open the back door, Parker raised the biscuit high. "Fetch!" he cried, hurling it into the yard.

In a shot, Boof blasted through the doorway, flour sack still clamped in his jaws. Parker slammed the door behind him and leaned his forehead against it.

How in the heck could he endure three months of taking care of this creature? Bamboo shoots under the finger-nails would be preferable. Or being frozen in carbonite, like Han Solo. At least that way he wouldn't be so aware of all this . . . chaos.

Parker's chest squeezed tight and his fingers twitched just thinking about the disaster Boof had made of the house. With a shudder, he inserted a panel to block the doggie door, collected the broom and dustpan, and went to work.

⇧⇩

After sweeping, vacuuming, and mopping up the down-stairs, Parker could finally relax. Order was restored.

Heaving a bone-deep sigh of relief, he started his homework. But soon a barking and scratching at the back door reminded him that his cleaning was far from over.

*Boof.*

Parker's head sank into his hands. If he wanted a clean house to stay clean, he'd have to bathe the dog.

He groaned. How exactly did you clean up a dog? Pelt them with water balloons? Chase them through a car wash? Usually Billie handled this stuff.

Parker retrieved a bucket from under the sink and filled it with soapy water, then lugged it outside. But after spilling most of it on his feet when Boof wouldn't hold still, Parker finally resorted to chasing the dog around with a hose and blasting him clean with the spray nozzle.

Later, after a hot shower and a change of clothes, Parker enjoyed two and a half hours of peace (apart from the howling). The soggy dog was outside, and he was inside.

Bliss.

Of course, his serenity crumbled after dinner, when his parents finally came home and made him bring Boof indoors. But you can't have everything.

Even so, the dog quieted down once he'd played ball with Parker's dad, and Parker dared to hope for a calm night.

He should have known better.

The family settled in to watch TV together—one of those rare times when neither of Parker's parents was working through the evening. But only fifteen minutes into the show, a great clatter and crash echoed from the dining room.

"What on earth?" asked his mom.

Parker was on his feet in a heartbeat. "I'll go check."

By now, he was expecting to discover that Boof had created some fresh mess, but the sight that greeted him left Parker dumbstruck.

On the shelves of the hutch, the Pitts family kept some of its dearest treasures—dusty heirlooms, framed photos, and mementos from special vacations—including the last gift Mimi had given Parker, the carved statue of the trickster Eshu.

She'd shared some of the legends about the Orisha deities (nearly as exciting as the *Star Wars* saga), and boasted that the Pitts family could trace its roots back to that Yoruba part of West Africa. Parker cherished the statue. True, he couldn't keep it in his room anymore because it made him too sad, but he still liked to admire it sometimes.

Somehow, Boof had reared up on his hind legs and swept a shelf clean, knocking several photos, a German beer stein, and the carving onto the floor. As Parker watched in horror, the dog braced the statue between his paws and began chewing on it.

White teeth sank into rich brown iroko.

The wood crunched.

At the sound, Parker's pulse throbbed in his ears, and his vision narrowed to a red tunnel.

*"No!"* he roared, charging forward. Before Boof could escape with his prize, Parker clutched the carving's other end in a death grip. "Give it, you lousy dog!"

Back and forth they tugged. Neither had the advantage; neither would let go. But with each yank, the golden-doodle's teeth scarred the statue more and more.

Destroying his grandma's keepsake. Erasing her memory.

"Drop it!" Parker growled.

Boof growled back, tail waggling.

Parker's jaw clenched. For a moment, all the fine hairs stood up on his body. He felt wobbly inside, like he was looking down from the top of the world's tallest Ferris wheel.

Then a blast of heat roared through him, relentless as a forest fire. That was *it*—the last straw.

Boof had wrecked Billie's farewell dinner, he'd trashed the house, and now he was destroying Parker's last memento of Mimi. In that instant, Parker wished that Boof had to deal with a rotten, no-good, misbehaving dog, so *he* could see how it felt.

In a flash, it seemed as though his anger had somehow flowed into the carving. For an endless second, the wood radiated heat like a fireplace poker. Boof yipped. Parker cried out. Releasing the statue at the same instant, both of them tumbled backward.

*Clonk* went Parker's head against the dining room table; Boof skidded back into the wall. Another wave of nausea rippled through Parker. When it had gone, he retrieved the carving (now as cool as ever) and probed the sore spot on the back of his head.

"Look what you did!" he yelled at the dog, brandishing his statue.

Boof cringed. His gaze looked sorrowful.

From behind Parker, a deep voice rumbled, "I think someone needs a time-out."

"No kidding," said Parker. "This dog is totally out of control."

His dad cleared his throat. "I was talking about you."

"What?! Am I the only person who sees how bad this dog is acting?"

"He's not the only one."

The unfairness almost took Parker's breath away. "He

destroyed Mimi's statue! He's wrecking our house! Why doesn't anyone care but me?"

"You're being dramatic," said his father in a tight, controlled voice. "Go to your room. Now."

Parker's gut felt harder than steel. His hands trembled.

Without another word, he turned and stalked upstairs to his bedroom, grasping the statue in a white-knuckled grip. Maybe it was the aftereffects of his encounter, but he felt off-balance, dizzy, not quite in his right mind.

Parker flopped onto the bed, muttering to himself.

Nobody was on his side. Nobody knew how hard it was being him.

Well, fine. Parker would show them.

He'd show them all.

Somehow, some way, soon everyone—including that rotten dog Boof—would know exactly how he felt.

# PARKER ⇨

## 4

## Dog's-Eye View

Just before the alarm clock chimed, a symphony of smells pulled Parker from a strange dream about chasing squirrels. Sizzling bacon, the bitter richness of coffee, yeasty sourdough toast about to burn—he smelled it all in high-def and 4-D. Even stronger came the funk of T-shirts in his laundry hamper, the reek of someone's armpits, and a whiff of hot chocolate from that spill he'd wiped up last week.

All those scents and more shoved their way into his nose like an opening-day crowd at Comic-Con.

He sneezed.

*Bee-beep, bee-beep, bee-beep*, the clock yammered.

With a jaw-cracking yawn, Parker opened his eyes and stretched. He blinked, then blinked again.

Like something seen through one of the more boring Instagram filters, his dim bedroom appeared pure gray. But that wasn't what bothered him.

Something didn't make sense.

Instead of facing his neatly ordered bedside table with its clock and water glass, Parker was gazing up at his bed from a low angle. He stared.

At the arm dangling off it.

At himself, sleeping.

*Bee-beep, bee-beep, bee-beep.* The clock kept ringing.

*Still dreaming.* Parker shook his head, trying to wake up. As he did, something whapped gently against his cheeks. He raised a hand to investigate, and a paw appeared instead.

"Gah!"

He flinched. At the same time, some part of Parker's brain registered that he'd heard an odd chuffing sound instead of a "gah."

*What the heck was happening?*

Up he surged—and found himself on all fours. Looking down, Parker saw not his own feet but two furry legs ending in paws.

"Augh!" he cried. But it came out as a bark.

*Holy crud! I'm a* dog*?!*

He was stuck in the freakiest dream ever. And the alarm clock just kept blaring.

The figure on the bed stirred. "Chase the birds," it mumbled.

Parker reeled. He couldn't seem to catch a breath. That

was *him* speaking—his voice coming from his mouth—but he wasn't saying the words.

Was he going completely wackadoodle?

"I-I'm dreaming," he told himself. "No big deal. Just, someone else is in my body. And I've got . . . paws." But his voice came out in a growly whine.

The boy on the bed jerked upright. "What?"

With a gasp, Parker realized that the walls, the bed, the desk, the boy—*everything* was painted in shades of gray, save a few yellows and blues.

Something was seriously wrong with his eyes. Or his brain.

Could he have a tumor? Was he going to die like Mimi?

Over on the bed, the boy with Parker's face examined his hands in horror. "Paws!" he cried.

"That's right, genius," Parker growled. "I've got four of them!"

"No, *my* paws," said the boy. "They look weird!" Bringing a palm to his nose, he took a deep whiff. "And my sniffer is broken!" he wailed.

*Bee-beep, bee-beep, bee-beep.* The clock rang on, as relentless as a toddler asking *why*. Parker clenched his jaws. His head was about to explode. The harsh beeping, the doggie body, the boy who looked like him—it was all too much.

*"Aaaagh!"* they cried together, Parker's voice emerging as a mournful howl.

From downstairs, a deep voice boomed, "What's going on up there?"

"Nothing, Dad!" Parker called. But all that came out was more barking.

"Are you horsing around with Boof?" his dad shouted. "Turn off that alarm clock and hop to it."

*No, no, no, this can't be happening,* Parker thought. *Wake up, wake up!*

He went to pinch himself awake. But you can't pinch with paws. Instead, Parker bit down hard on his tongue to break up the nightmare, but all that happened was pain.

"Yikes!"

"Holy possum poop!" the boy with his face moaned. "My eyes! Too many colors!" He clapped his hands over his eyes, swung his legs off the bed, stood, and face-planted with a *whump.* All the action knocked something off the bed and onto the floor.

Parker blinked. It was the statue they'd been fighting over last night.

"And what's with my mouth?" the fake Parker marveled, rolling onto his back. "It's talking human words. Look at me! Blah, blah, blah, cats are stupid!"

Great. Parker was trapped in his room with a total nutjob.

"Bird?" His dad's voice sounded closer now. Strangely, Parker could already smell him through the closed door: a mix of aftershave, Old Spice deodorant, and manly musk. "Stop messing around and get ready for school. You hear me?"

*Uh-oh.* No way could Dad enter this room right now.

"Hey, you." Parker swatted the boy with a paw. "Say, 'Okay, Dad.'"

"Okay, Dad," the boy repeated, pushing up to sitting. "Okay, okay, okay, okay . . ." He looked dazed.

Parker slapped a paw over the nutjob's mouth. But he knew how the boy was feeling. His own head was spinning like a show-off skater in the Olympic finals.

"Everything all right in there?" asked his dad. *Why won't he leave?*

"Just fine," said Parker. Removing his paw, he nudged the boy to repeat after him.

"Fine, fine, fine!" The boy's voice pitched from low to high, experimenting with tone. Parker had to jam his shoulder into the fake Parker's mouth to get him to stop. Turning his face away, the boy spat doggie hair.

A long pause from the other side of the door. Parker held his breath. The boy picked up a discarded tennis shoe with his mouth and gave it a few tentative chews.

"All right, little man," said his father's voice at last. "Shake a leg. Breakfast is almost ready." His footsteps receded.

Parker frowned at the boy wearing his face. "What gives?"

Spitting out the shoe, the boy cocked his head in a dog-like gesture. "Huh?"

"How come he can't understand me, but you can?"

The fake Parker shot him an odd look. "I speak Dog. What else would I speak?"

Right. Clearly this kid had hit his head on something hard.

On its own, the alarm clock finally stuttered and stopped. In the sudden quiet, Parker tried to get a grip on his situation.

"Hey, um, you." The boy broke into his thoughts.

"Yeah?"

"How come you're in my body?"

Parker chuffed. "*Your* body? Who the heck are you?"

"Everyone calls me Boof," said the boy with Parker's face. He held up a hand before his eyes, twisting it this way and that. "Wow. Fingers."

A sudden coldness struck at Parker's core, like he'd just swallowed a pint of peppermint ice cream. *"You're—?"* He gasped. *No, it isn't possible. These things don't just happen.* "I'm—?" As the realization struck, Parker's back legs wobbled and he sat with a *whump.* "What the heck are we doing in each other's bodies?" he wailed.

Boof cocked his head, considering. "Well . . ."

"Yes?"

"No idea."

Around the room Parker paced, his skin prickling as the reality sank in. A *dog*? No way. He couldn't be a dog. Dogs were filthy creatures, teeming with disease. They ate poop. They drank from the toilet bowl. At this very moment, fleas, ticks, and who knew what else could be crawling all over him.

The thought made him want to stand under a piping-hot shower for an hour.

Parker shook himself vigorously. "Gross! I can't be in a dog's body."

"You're lucky," said Boof.

*"Lucky?!"*

"You're a dog, which is awesome."

"That's—"

"Look at *me,*" said Boof. "My nose is shot, my eyes are all wacko, and I'm stuck in this short human shape."

"I am *not* short!" Parker's hackles bristled. "I was the twelfth-tallest kid in my class last year."

Light dawned in Boof's eyes. "Ah, you're Gloomy Boy?"

"'Gloomy Boy?'" said Parker. "No. I'm NOT gloomy!"

Boof nodded. Raising a hand, he gave it a tentative lick, as if he were testing an unfamiliar food. "Yep, Gloomy Boy, all right. So we, like, swapped?"

"I—uh, yes," said Parker. "Unless I'm hallucinating all this." He closed his eyes. "Please let it be a brain tumor."

Boof whooped. "All right!"

"Are you completely cocoa bananas? This stinks."

The boy sniffed. "Really? I don't smell anything. Of course, my nose is messed up."

"No, I mean, *this is awful*. What? Why are you still smiling?"

"I just realized." Boof's grin spread even wider. "If I'm human, I can get inside that cold metal thingy full of food."

"The fridge?" said Parker.

"Oh, yeah," said Boof, crawling for the door. "Sweet fringe, here I come!"

Parker's whole body tingled with alarm. Scampering around in front of Boof, he bared his teeth. "Stop!"

"Why?"

"You can't just crawl around on all fours."

"Why not?" asked Boof. "I always do."

With a growl, Parker said, "But you're in *my* body now. *I* walk on two feet."

Boof shrugged. "I'll say I got bored."

He reached for the doorknob.

"No!" barked Parker.

Surprised, Boof sank back onto his haunches. "You don't have to shout."

"Trust me, if you crawl around the house, Mom and Dad will send you to a shrink."

"So, I get smaller," said Boof. "I'm already short."

"I'm NOT short."

Gritting his teeth, Parker hung his head. On top of everything else, he was arguing with a dog? He sucked in a deep breath.

"Going to the shrink is bad," he said. "Like going to the vet."

Boof's face (actually, Parker's own face—so weird to see that) blanched. "Ugh. Forget that." He reached up, seized the doorknob with both hands, and hauled himself to his feet.

Parker backed away as the boy swayed to and fro.

"Gack!" Boof frowned down at his new legs. "How do you balance on these things?"

"I don't know," said Parker. "I've had twelve years of practice."

"Four legs make much more sense." Releasing the doorknob, Boof teetered, trying to stand on his own.

"Never mind," barked Parker. "We've got to work on switching ourselves back."

Boof blinked down at him. "Okeydokey," he said. "*After* I raid the fringe." And with that, he twisted the knob, pulled open the door, and reeled into the hall.

"It's called a *fridge*," said Parker. "Stop right there!"

His grab missed. This paw thing was going to take some getting used to. Chasing after the lurching Boof, he managed to catch a mouthful of pajama leg.

"Whoops!" Boof clutched the banister, just barely staying upright.

"Come back here," Parker growled around the fabric.

Boof pulled away. Parker tugged back.

"Don't wanna." Boof pouted. "Wanna have some *fun*." He yanked his leg harder, the pajamas ripped, and Parker tumbled back onto his haunches.

"Look what you did." Parker spat out a scrap of fabric. "Will you get back in this room before you totally blow it?"

Boof raised his hands, palms up. "What's the problem?"

"The *problem?*" Parker narrowed his eyes. "I want my

body back. And if you act like a dog while you're inside it, my parents will pack me—you—off to an insane asylum."

A goofy smile played across Boof's face. "What, you don't think I can act human?" He scratched behind his ear with a vigorous, doglike motion.

Parker stared pointedly.

"What?"

"You wouldn't last ten minutes as me," said Parker.

"Ha! Dogs study humans all the time," said Boof. "We're practically human experts."

"Right."

"Look, here's you." Boof wrinkled his nose, adopting a prissy tone. "Eeew, dirt bad. Poop bad. Dog very bad."

Parker snorted. "That's not me."

Waving off his comment, Boof said, "I can do you better than you can."

"In your dreams! You can barely stand."

With a haughty look, Boof released the banister and took several steps toward the head of the stairs. He wobbled, but he didn't fall. "See? Dogs learn quick."

"Sure you do," said Parker. "It took you three weeks to remember to pee outdoors."

"Ooh, that reminds me," said Boof. "This body says it's 'go' time." Spinning on his heel and nearly toppling over, he tottered down the hallway to the bathroom. "See? I know where to go."

"Do you even know how to use the toilet?" Parker scrambled to catch up.

As they entered, his nose wrinkled in disgust. *Whew.* The bathroom *reeked.* Who'd have ever guessed it was this filthy? He fought the urge to break out the cleanser and a sponge.

"What's to know?" said Boof. "You point and shoot." Stepping up to the toilet, he pushed down his pajama bottoms.

Even though he was looking at his own body, Parker felt a rush of squeamishness and turned away. The splash of water on porcelain followed quickly.

"See?" said Boof. "Easy as digging a hole."

Parker turned back to witness Boof spraying the toilet seat and surrounding area as he swayed on his feet. "No, no, no!" Parker cried. "*In* the bowl, not around it. Gross!"

Yanking up the pajama pants, Boof lurched toward the hallway. "Time to eat. I'm hungry!"

"No! Wash your hands and clean up this mess!"

"Why?"

"It's what humans do."

Boof snorted. "Don't wanna."

With a wave of nausea, Parker surveyed the wet floor and toilet seat. What a disaster! He bit down on the end of the toilet paper roll and backed away until he'd unwound a substantial length. Tearing it off, he dropped the wad of paper on the floor. "Disgusting."

Leaning on the doorframe, Boof said, "Let's see you do better in my body."

"Eeww, eeww, *eeww*." Parker shoved the toilet paper around with one paw, trying to mop up the spill without stepping in the puddle. It was impossible.

Boof sniffed the air. "Mmm, cooked pig." And in a blink, he was gone.

"Wait!" cried Parker. He wavered. Could he pick up the damp toilet paper without using his mouth? Nope, couldn't be done. "Argh!"

Parker wheeled, chasing after Boof.

As he entered the hallway, Parker saw the boy swaying toward the top of the stairs.

*No!*

He raced after Boof, a distant part of his mind noticing, *Hey, this dog body is a strong one*. He felt agile, coordinated, fast. If he'd been this together at football tryouts, he'd have made the team for sure. Then Parker registered what was happening with his human body, and his eyes widened.

Boof stood above the first step. One foot lifted.

"Careful!" cried Parker, as quietly as he could.

"No worries," said Boof. "Walking is easy."

Wearing a huge grin, he stepped down onto the first step, lost his balance, and tumbled headlong down a full flight of stairs.

PARKER ⇨

# 5

# Floor Toast

Wild with worry, Parker galloped down the steps. Negotiating stairs on four legs sure felt weird, but that experience paled beside seeing his own body huddled on the landing.

"Are you okay?" he cried.

"Ow," said the dog in human form. "Stairs hurt."

Parker's dad leaned through the kitchen doorway. "What was that noise?"

Boof blinked up at him, rising to his knees. "Oh, uh . . ."

"Did you fall?" Parker's dad came closer, a bread knife and a plate of half-buttered toast in his hands. "Are you okay?"

"Get up!" Parker nudged the boy with his snout. "Tell him you're fine."

At the sight of food, Boof bounced to his feet, leaned forward, and snatched a slice of toast from the plate with his mouth.

"Hey!" said Dad.

If he hadn't been so upset, Parker would've laughed out loud at the expression on his father's face.

Boof beamed as he chewed. "I'm—*mmf*—fiiine."

"Ooh-kay." Sending him a strange look, Parker's dad returned to the kitchen.

"You've got to be more careful," Parker said when his father had gone. "Don't break my body before I can get it back."

Boof barely heard. He'd rolled up a sleeve and was busy trying to lick the reddish bump on his elbow where he'd whacked it on a step. His tongue wouldn't reach, so he licked his opposite hand's fingers and rubbed them over the injury.

"Food time!" he chirped. And with that, he swayed off into the kitchen. With a heavy sigh, Parker followed.

This was going to be an epic disaster.

Breakfast aromas invaded his nose, and Parker felt his mouth water like a summer sprinkler. The bacon smell was so intense and rich; he swore he could tell which farm the pig came from and what it last had to eat.

Golden morning light flooded the kitchen. That looked pretty much the same as usual, but the normally tangerine walls were a kind of grayish yellow and the green ficus in the corner a light gray.

Parker moaned, shaking his head. His new eyes were giving him a headache.

"What's with the dog?" His dad placed two singed pieces of toast on a plate with eggs and bacon, and handed it to Boof. "Is he missing Billie?"

After nearly dropping his breakfast, Boof figured out how to use his hands properly. "Oh. Him? He, uh, got up on the wrong side of the bed." Smirking at Parker, Boof stalked with exaggerated care to the breakfast table.

Parker felt like biting Boof's leg. How could he take everything so lightly? They were stuck in the wrong bodies with no clue how to reverse things, and here he was, joking around.

Collapsing into a chair, Boof lowered his face to the plate and began scarfing up bacon like an industrial vacuum.

"Hands!" Parker darted a glance to see if his father had noticed Boof's behavior, but he was returning things to the fridge.

Through a mouthful of bacon, Boof mumbled, "Hands?"

"Eat like a human," said Parker, "with your hands and a fork."

"How's that?" asked his dad, turning to Boof.

"Um . . . hands?" said the boy.

Parker's father quirked an eyebrow. "What about them?"

Wiggling his fingers, Boof said, "They don't look much like paws."

"Riiight," said Parker's dad. "Eat up, Birdman, time's a-wasting." He carried the skillets to the sink, squirted them with soap, and turned on the faucet.

Parker's gut twisted. It was weird to hear his dad calling Boof by his special nickname. He felt oddly left out. With Mimi around, Parker had known where he fit in this family. With her gone—and with this bizarre change—he wasn't so sure.

Jamming two slices of bacon into his mouth at once, Boof munched and crunched with delight. True, he wasn't using a fork, but at least he'd picked up the strips instead of slurping them directly off the plate.

*This is crazy*, Parker reflected. *How did it happen? Was it my fault—something I did?*

Watching Boof eat made his own stomach growl like a bad-tempered bear coming out of hibernation. "How about some bacon?" he asked.

"Why? You never share with me."

Parker's response came out as a cross between a grunt and a *woof*. "Come *on*. I'm hungry."

Still washing dishes, his dad remarked over his shoulder, "Boof sure has a lot to say today."

"He's begging," said Boof-in-Parker's-body. "Dog food's

not good enough anymore." He stuck out his tongue at Parker.

Parker bristled. "You give me some bacon right now." Drool fountained from his mouth—*gross*—and he tried to wipe it off with a paw.

Breaking off a chunk of toast with his fingers, Boof held it aloft. "You better sit."

Parker's eyes narrowed and a low growl emerged from his throat.

"Come on, doggie-woggie," said Boof, waving the toast fragment. "You know how to sit, don't you?"

*Ugh.* This was unbearable. But the breakfast smells were driving him nuts and he just *had* to eat. Grumbling, Parker sat.

"Good boy!" chirped Boof, tossing the bread.

Parker snapped at it, and the toast bounced off his nose, landing on the floor.

*Oh, no!*

He stared at it. Not a fan of the three-second rule, Parker felt that eating anything once it had touched the floor was super-gross.

Meanwhile, Boof continued wolfing down his breakfast. Using the rest of the toast to scoop scrambled eggs into his gullet, he chomped with his mouth open, spraying food flecks right and left. Parker would've worried about the mess, but his hunger trumped everything.

"Give me another piece," he said.

"Can you shake?" said Boof, holding out a hand. "Or roll over?"

Parker wanted to howl in frustration. How could he eat off that filthy floor? But if the alternative was dog food . . .

Peeling back his lips in disgust, he extended his snout to within an inch of the toast. The rich butter smell and the tang of singed sourdough filled his nostrils, along with dirt, shoe leather, spilled orange juice, and that lemony stuff his parents used to clean the floor.

He'd have been so much happier smelling less.

Ignorance is bliss.

With great reluctance, Parker caught the toast between his teeth, then realized he couldn't take civilized bites without dropping it back onto the floor. *Ugh.* Having no hands was such a drag. Sinking onto his belly, he clamped the toast between his forepaws and bit off a piece.

It was like someone had coated his tongue with varnish. He could taste the bread somewhat, but nowhere near as vividly as he could smell it. Dog taste buds were seriously lacking.

*Human* taste buds, on the other hand . . .

"Mmm, yum, oh, *wow.*" Boof snarfed up the last of his

eggs. "This is better than premium Alpo! I've never tasted anything so good."

Parker's dad made a wry face. "It's only bacon and eggs, and burnt toast. Your mom went to work early, and I can't cook like your grandmother used to." He sighed, glancing up at the ceiling. "Some days I miss her so much."

Parker felt sorrow well up in him like a rising tide.

The corners of his father's lips tugged downward, and Parker swore he could detect a sad *smell* coming off him. Was this what dogs experienced all the time? It was unnerving. He had more than enough of his own feelings to handle, without becoming hyperaware of his parents', thank you very much.

Parker gulped, turning away. He felt a strong urge to tidy up the kitchen. True, he couldn't do much with his paws. But he managed to pick up a canvas shopping bag that had fallen to the floor and loop its handle over the doorknob. It was a start.

His father gave him a strange look and cleared his throat. "Uh, why don't you let the dog out? He's probably bursting. And remember to feed and walk him before school."

Boof licked his plate. "No more food?"

"Stop messing around and do your chores," said Parker's dad. "I shouldn't have to tell you twice."

"Okay, okay," said Boof. Pushing off the tabletop, he rose to his feet and weaved toward the back door.

"Everything all right, there?" asked Parker's father.

"Hmm?" Boof turned a blank look his way.

Parker stiffened. "Say you're dizzy. Tell him you stood up too fast."

"Boof, be quiet!" said his dad. "Man, that dog is barky today."

"He just won't shut up," agreed Boof.

As Parker's dad busied himself clearing the dirty dishes, Boof made an awkward *come here* gesture. "Let's go, Dog." He reached the door and managed to turn the knob without falling over.

Now that push came to shove, Parker realized he actually did need to relieve himself, and soon. He wished he'd thought of that when they were upstairs in the bathroom.

Everything was happening way too fast.

As they entered the backyard, a storm of smells assaulted Parker's nose. The cool autumn air carried the scent of dying grass, jasmine blossoms, old dog poop that Billie had missed, oil from the neighbors' ancient Chevrolet, the Great Pyrenees dog next door, and a whole lot more. He sneezed, but that only intensified the odors.

Boof paused, taking a deep whiff. "Was that cat here again? I can't tell. *Pfft*, this nose."

Parker hustled into the bushes. If a dog's face could've blushed, his would have. How humiliating—not to mention unhygienic—to have to relieve himself outdoors. And just to leave it there? When he'd finished his business, Parker kicked dirt over it as best he could.

"You know," said Boof, coming up behind him, "that's more of a cat thing."

"I don't care!" snapped Parker. "Being a dog is nasty. How do you live like this?"

Boof shrugged. Spotting a scruffy old tennis ball, he perked up. "Hey!" He kicked the mangy thing to Parker. "Throw the ball?"

"I'd love to."

"Great!"

With his best doggie approximation of a sarcastic smile, Parker said, "As soon as I grow a pair of hands."

"Aw, come on. Ball!"

"We've got more important things to do."

Boof's expression was incredulous. "Like what?"

"Duh." Parker paced. "Reversing what's happened to us."

"But I haven't even explored that big white food box," Boof whined.

"Forget the fridge. You can feast from it once we're back in our normal bodies."

Boof's eyes brightened. "Promise?"

"Sure, whatever. Just help me think this through."

"Okay." Boof frowned, staring at a corner of the yard while he bit his lip.

"Just one question," he said at last.

"What's that?"

"How do I think?"

Parker rolled his eyes, surprised to find that it was just as easy to do in this dog body. "Help me remember last night. What was different?"

Squinting up into the maple tree, Boof ruffled his hair. "Uh . . . you washed me?"

"Besides that." Parker sat down on his doggie haunches. "You spread flour all over the house . . ."

"Fun!"

"And you were being difficult."

"No, I was just—" Boof stiffened, pointing at a low branch. "Ooh! Bird!"

"Forget the bird," said Parker. "Focus!"

But Boof was so distracted, Parker had to head-butt him to break his stare. At last, Boof looked down. "Huh?"

"Let's go step by step," said Parker. "We were watching TV, and then—"

"And then . . . aha! I saw the yummy stick."

Parker scowled. "Mimi's statue. We had a tug-of-war."

"Big fun," said Boof. "And then . . ."

Boy and dog frowned, stuck for a moment. "Things get kind of hazy after that," admitted Parker.

"Um . . . I remember falling down and bumping into something."

"Could that have done it?"

Boof shrugged again. "Don't ask me. I'm a dog."

"Let's try it."

Boof's expression was doubtful, but he crouched down. "So what do we pull on?"

Scanning the backyard, Parker spotted only one thing that would do the trick: a nasty, old blue rubber bone that was probably covered with bird poop, snail slime, and worse. He trotted over, shivered in disgust, and then gingerly picked it up in his teeth, trying not to smell the thing.

Parker returned to Boof. When the boy grabbed the other end, they locked eyes. "Okay, pull hard and then release it when I say go," said Parker around the bone in his mouth. "Pull!"

"Yeah!" said Boof, nearly yanking Parker off his feet. "This is more like it!"

Planting his forepaws, Parker tugged. They seesawed forward and back, neither maintaining the advantage for long.

"Okayyy," rumbled Parker. "One, two, three . . . *go*!"

At once, they released the chew toy, and—*whump!*—

tumbled backward onto the ground like two awkward acrobats.

Parker landed on a rock. "Ow!" A little breathless, he waited a handful of heartbeats. "Feel anything different?"

"Yeah."

"What?"

"My butt hurts." Rolling onto one side, Boof rubbed his behind.

Parker slumped. Nothing had changed. They were both still stuck in the wrong bodies.

The back door swung open. "Hey, little man! Stop rolling around and get the lead out," said Parker's dad. "You've still got to feed him and get ready for school."

"Sorry, Dad," said Parker automatically. When he realized his father couldn't understand him and wouldn't until this condition changed, his vision blurred. He was like a ghost in his own home.

Boof just waved.

But after Parker's father went inside, Boof turned to Parker with dawning alarm on his face.

"School?" he asked.

"School." Parker sighed a deep doggie sigh. He could see about six different ways this might play out, and none of them ended well.

# 6

# Mrs. Stinky Flower

This was *awesome*—better than a brand-new chew toy. Boof had never gotten to ride in the car's front seat before. He hopped about and hung his head out the window, letting the whoosh of cool air blow all the glorious scents into his nose. True, he could barely smell anything with this weird human sniffer, and his ears didn't flap in the breeze like they used to.

But still—car ride!

"Seat belts, buddy," said Ball Man, glancing over at him as they rolled down the road.

"Seat belts," said Boof. Back and forth he swiveled, spotting blue jays, cats, squirrels, people walking other dogs. So much to see!

"Bird—" the man began.

"Where?" Boof swiveled his head.

Parker's dad frowned. "Stop messing around, son. Buckle

up." He pointed at the strappy thing hanging beside Boof's shoulder.

"Oh. Okay." Boof had watched the humans work these gizmos before. Let's see . . . you pulled the belt away from the window, and . . . He glanced at the father's strappy thing for a clue, and his own belt slipped from his grip and whipped back against the car door.

Human hands were super-weird. And so sensitive. He was still getting the hang of using them.

Once more, he tugged on the strap, and this time he managed to slip its end into the slot on the seat's far side. Success! Boof felt his butt move, but he had no glorious tail to wag.

This would take some getting used to.

"Did you hear me?" asked Ball Man.

He had been saying something, but Boof hadn't been listening. He asked the man to repeat himself.

"Where's your head at this morning?" asked Parker's dad. Boof pointed to it. Maybe the man's eyesight wasn't so great. "You seem a little out of it today, Birdman. Rough night?"

Boof's eyebrows rose. "You could say that."

"Remember, Cody's mom will pick you guys up today. I've got a meeting and your mother's working late."

"Uh, sure," said Boof. He never particularly liked it

when people picked him up, but the Boy had advised him to go along with things while he was pretending to be Parker. Boof did remember the one called Cody, who always smelled of corn chips and cat, and was willing to share his snacks with a hungry dog. Cody was all right.

All too soon, Ball Man stopped the car before a cluster of wide buildings where many kids milled about. Boof watched them emerging from other cars and pouring through the gate. Everyone seemed to be in a hurry—another common human problem.

"Okay, buddy. Enjoy your day," said Parker's dad.

"I always do."

A few moments passed as Boof watched the scene outside.

"Okay, son."

"Okay," said Boof. Some of those kids were actually running toward the buildings. Why? Was someone handing out Snausages inside?

"Stop messing around and get out." Ball Man seemed impatient. Had Boof done something wrong? "Go on inside; I have to get to work."

After fumbling with the seat belt, Boof finally managed to release the strap. The car door gave him some trouble, but he figured that out too, and soon he stood on the sidewalk.

He was hoping maybe the man would reward him with a treat for his cleverness, but Parker's father merely held up a bag by its strap, saying, "Forget something?"

The bag was heavy, smelling of books and ink. But the Boy had told him to carry it around today, so Boof slipped his arms through the loops and hefted it onto his back.

*Ugh.* Why would anyone willingly lug anything this bulky? Dogs always traveled light.

Passing through the gate and the main building's double doors, he found himself constantly swiveling his head. Kids and grownups of every shape and size streamed around him, gabbing and waving their arms about like a flock of ditzy ducks at the lake.

So many bright colors! So much action! Boof's eyes were dazzled. He longed to put a nose to these passing strangers and investigate them. Not that this new nose would help much. He missed his good old sniffer.

But still, he was at school! Now at least he'd solve the mystery of what Gloomy Boy and Sweet Girl did every day for so long.

In their hasty briefing before leaving the house, the Boy had pointed to a piece of paper in the bag that he said would tell Boof where he needed to go and when. But then Ball Man had hauled him off before Boof could remind

Parker that he didn't understand those black marks on the sheet.

So . . . where to go?

Making the most of his limited senses, Boof took a deep whiff. Faint odors of fruity shampoo, marking pens, and baking bread reached his nostrils. No lingering scent trails of Gloomy Boy, no clue where to go. Boof stopped dead in the middle of the human tide, scratching his head.

How did people ever find their way around with such weak sniffers?

"Parker!" someone called. "Yo, Parker! You awake?"

With a start, Boof recalled he was supposed to answer to that name. He turned, and the light-haired boy called Cody made a *come-here* gesture.

"Did aliens eat your brain?" said Cody. Up close, Boof noticed that the boy had a round face like a pug. "Come on, dude!"

Boof joined him, wondering what aliens were. (And for that matter, a brain.) Gloomy Boy had told him to stick close to Cody, since they were in most of the same classes together (whatever those were). As was customary, Boof bent to sniff the boy's crotch in greeting.

"Whoa!" Cody shoved him away. "Back off, brah. What's wrong with you?"

"I, uh, got Amelia."

Cody frowned. "Amelia?"

"Yeah." The Boy had told him to say that, in case anyone questioned his behavior. But maybe it wasn't quite the right word. "Um, Artesia? Rhodesia?"

Now Cody was staring at him like he had four tails. *Grmph*. This was so frustrating.

"You know," said Boof. "That thing you get when you hit your head?"

Cody's face cleared. "Amnesia?"

"Yeah, that!" cried Boof. He was so relieved, he jumped forward and licked the boy's face.

"Jeez Louise!" Cody swabbed his cheek with a forearm, pushing Boof back. "You really are cuckoo for Cocoa Puffs. Friends don't lick friends."

"Oh," said Boof. Did this boy not like him anymore? Boof really wanted to be liked.

"It's okay, dude." Cody steered him down the hall through the river of tall kids. "You really hit your head? Seriously?"

"Yeah."

"You gonna be okay?"

That was an excellent question. Boof didn't know the answer, but he was a hopeful dog, so he said, "Yes?"

"Good." Cody wheeled them around a knot of giggling girls. "On what?"

"Huh?"

The boy waved a hand. "What did you hit your head on?"

"Oh. The, um, table," said Boof.

"Ow." Cody grimaced. "And so now you can't remember stuff?"

Squinching up his face, Boof nodded. He felt a little funny telling this story, even though Gloomy Boy had ordered him to. After all, he could remember things just fine. He knew where he'd buried that old beef bone in the backyard, which pocket Parker's father usually kept his treats in, and where that mean cat from the corner house liked to hang out.

But the Boy had told him that in the human world, you sometimes needed to say stuff that was a little bit . . . not true.

One of many things Boof didn't get about humans.

As they rounded the corner, he bumped into a girl. She staggered, off-balance. He caught an arm to steady her.

"Thanks," she said with a sweet smile.

Boof smiled back.

The girl reminded him of a spaniel. She was pretty, for a human, with loads of shiny dark hair, and she smelled amazing, like flowers and peaches and fresh-baked pies.

His human body felt all tingly. Boof started to bend forward to sniff her, but Cody steadied him with a hand to the shoulder.

"He's sorry," said Cody, looking from the girl to her curly-haired friend.

"No, I'm not," said Boof, still grinning at Peach Girl. "You're so pretty. I could bump into you all day long."

Curly Hair gasped and covered her mouth. Peach Girl giggled, her cheeks reddening. "Stop!" she said, swatting Boof's arm.

He stopped, a little confused.

Cody's jaw dropped.

"You're, um, Parker, right?" said the girl.

"For today, anyway," said Boof.

Peach Girl giggled again. "I'm Gabi. At the moment."

"You're fun," said Boof. "Want to get together sometime and play Sniff the Butts?"

Cody gasped.

"I don't know that one." Gabi's face lit up. "But how did you know I'm a gamer?"

Not having a clue what she meant, Boof just shrugged. She seemed nice, like the type of girl who would happily throw the ball for him.

"I'd like that," said Gabi.

Curly Hair frowned at their conversation, tugging on

Peach Girl's arm. "Well, that's all totally fascinating, but we've got to go . . ."

"Bye," said Boof. He'd heard humans say that when leaving.

"Bye," said Gabi. She held his gaze for a moment before they walked away.

Cody flapped his arms. "Dude! I can't believe you."

"What?" They resumed walking down the hall.

"Did that head bump totally change your personality? That's more words than you've said to Gabi in two years."

"Is it?"

Shaking his head, Cody said, "Calling her pretty? Flirting? Inviting her to *hang out*?"

Boof's brow furrowed. "And that's . . . bad?"

Bopping his shoulder, Cody said, "Are you kidding? That's epic! You're like, the bravest guy in sixth grade—braver than that kid who put out the dumpster fire."

"Really?" Boof didn't see what all the fuss was about. "I just told the truth."

"Dude, who does that?"

"Um . . ."

"Nobody! They're gonna be putting up statues of you."

Since he didn't know quite what to say, Boof decided he was better off saying nothing. After a few more comments, Cody settled down, leading the way into a room that, even to Boof's human nose, smelled of old paper, peanut butter, and marking pens.

Boof sneezed. And then he caught a faint scent that held far more interest than school stuff. His eyes scanned the room, past desks, past kids sitting or standing, and finally settled on a cage near the bank of windows.

"Bird!" Boof stiffened, pointing at the yellow-and-green creature on its perch.

"Uh, yeah," said Cody. He gently pushed Boof's hand down. "It's been there since the school year started."

"Oh." Boof's attention remained riveted on the little bird.

"Look, am I gonna have to watch out for you all day?" asked Cody. "You're like some weird mix of brilliant and clueless. Like Scooby-Doo."

"I, um—"

Whatever Boof had been planning to say, it was chopped off by a brain-piercing ringing. He clapped his hands over his ears.

The kids who'd been standing around, talking, sauntered over to their desks. As Cody guided Boof to a seat and told him to drop his bag on the floor, a tall, pear-shaped woman with a wrinkly bulldog face shuffled through the doorway, coming to a stop at the front of the room.

Even from four seats back, Boof could smell the sickly

sweet perfume the woman wore, like a rotting gardenia in a trash can. Dropping her enormous purse onto a cluttered desk, Mrs. Stinky Flower surveyed the students. Judging by the look on her face, she'd rather be anywhere—even on an examining table at the vet's—but there in that room.

"All right, quiet down, everyone," the woman droned. "You know the drill, so stand up."

Mystified, Boof rose to his feet with the rest of the students.

A box high on the wall crackled, making him jump, and a woman's cheerful voice emerged from it. "Good morning, Timberwolves! Today is Monday, October eleventh, and Bitsy Moon will lead us in the Pledge of Allegiance. Bitsy?"

A small voice as squeaky as a toy poodle's bark said, "Ready? Begin. I pledge allegiance . . . to the flag . . ."

Glancing about him, Boof noticed that the other students had placed a hand on their chests and were mumbling something together. Cody shot him a significant look, so he put his own hand to his chest and moved his lips.

Before long, everyone sat down again.

The yellow bird chirped, so Boof strolled over to inspect it more closely. If that shifty little feathered prisoner tried to make a break, he'd be all over it.

"Something urgent, Mr. Pitts?" asked Mrs. Stinky Flower.

Boof kept staring.

"Parker?" the woman said.

Boof realized she was talking to him. "That bird," he said. "I don't trust it."

In a voice like tires grinding on a gravel driveway, the woman said, "Winnie's fine. Take a seat." She pointed at the desk Boof had abandoned.

When Boof glanced at Cody, the boy nodded. He went and sat down again.

Through all this, the voice from the box kept squawking, finally wishing everyone a good morning and closing with a last crackle. Then Mrs. Stinky Flower began saying names that kids responded to with "here" or "present."

Honestly, who cared? Boof ignored this foolishness because he'd just caught the faint whiff of ham. Was it coming from the boy to his left? The girl in front?

Shifting in his seat, he flared his nostrils in vain. Darn this weak nose! Someone had meat, and he wouldn't rest until—

"Parker Pitts? Are you here?" The tall woman was staring at him. And now that he noticed, so were many of the other kids. Cody raised his eyebrows, nodding encouragingly.

"Oh," said Boof at last. "I'm not someplace else, so I must be here."

Kids snickered. The boy to his left who maybe had ham rolled his eyes.

"If you won't pay attention during roll call, Mr. Pitts, when will you?" asked the teacher.

"During feeding time," said Boof.

This got a big laugh.

"Is it soon?" Boof asked. More laughter, which puzzled him. "Seriously."

The woman's lips compressed into a hard line. "Lunch comes a lot sooner to those who stop disrupting class."

Sitting up straight in his chair, Boof tried his best to look like someone who wasn't disrupting class. (Whatever that looked like.) As far as he was concerned, this "lunch" couldn't come quickly enough. He was *always* hungry.

Mrs. Stinky Flower finished reciting names. Then she began discussing something called multiplication with fractions, which was so insanely boring that Boof soon returned his attention to that elusive ham smell.

He sniffed harder. The yummy aroma was almost certainly coming from the long-haired girl in front of him. Boof leaned closer, closer still . . .

"Mrs. Scales," said the girl, "Parker is sniffing my hair."

The woman's scowl looked weary. "Mr. Pitts, what did I say about disrupting class?"

"I forget," said Boof.

"And why are you sniffing Miss Martinez's hair?"

Boof grinned. "It smells like ham. The honey-glazed kind."

The roar of laughter that followed was enough to get Boof sent to the principal's office for the first time that day. But as he would soon discover, it wouldn't be the last.

PARKER ⇨

# 7

# The Golden Growls

"You *what?*" Parker demanded, after Boof had been dropped off at home and told him about his day at school.

"Saw the principal," said Boof. "Three whole times."

Over and over, Parker thumped his doggie head against the armchair. "Oh, my God. I'm so dead, I'm *so* dead."

"What's wrong with visiting the principal?" Boof shrugged. "There were cookies in the office."

Parker's lip curled back. "It's a bad thing."

"Cookies?"

"Being sent to the principal. That's where trouble-makers go."

Boof frowned. "I'm a troublemaker?"

"No, *I* am," said Parker. "That's what everyone will think now. I'm so dead."

"But why?"

Parker huffed out a breath. How to explain to Boof?

"Disrupting class? Cracking people up? Talking back to teachers? That's causing trouble."

"Oh. I see." The expression on Boof's face said he didn't see at all.

"And if you keep it up, they'll probably dock my grades. *Ugh.*" Parker flopped down onto the floor. "I'll never live this down. That's assuming I ever get my body back."

Squatting down, Boof frowned in sympathy and stroked the fur along his spine.

The petting felt good. But even as his body relaxed, Parker's thoughts chased one another like X-wing fighters on maneuvers. First, Miles moved away. Then Mimi died. Then Billie left, and now this, this . . . *situation* . . .

A bubble of sadness as big as a volleyball swelled up in his chest, and he moaned.

Boof rubbed his ruff. "Aw, it'll be okay, you'll see."

Grateful for Boof's comfort, Parker began to lean into the hand. Then he caught himself and broke away. "*How* will it be okay?"

Boof shrugged, offering a goofy grin. "I dunno. It just will."

Parker gave a disgusted *woof.*

Suddenly, Boof's face lit up. "Hey, the fridge! Now I can finally see what's inside." Without another word, he stood and marched into the kitchen.

"Wait!"

Trailing behind, Parker wrestled with a host of emotions. And the whirlwind of smells that assaulted his nose every second only made things worse.

Like now, as he passed by the chair where Mimi used to sit and found it drenched in her sandalwood perfume, triggering a wave of memories. Mimi teaching him tarot, talking *Star Wars* versus *Lord of the Rings*, opening his eyes to unseen energies, and generally making him feel like he wasn't such a freak.

It was all too much. Parker felt a sharp urge to tidy things.

Over to Boof's crate he trotted. Tugging and patting the sleeping pad with his paws, Parker made it as tidy as a doggie bed could be. Next, he turned to organizing the chew toys, lining them up from smallest to largest.

Beyond that, there wasn't much that a kid in a dog's body could do.

Parker sighed.

Meanwhile, Boof had yanked open the fridge and was randomly sniffing items and tossing them onto the counter.

"What's all this?" asked Parker.

"Snack time," said Boof. He peeled back the lid of a Tupperware container and smelled its contents. "Mmm, noodles!" Thrusting his face into the bowl, he scarfed up the leftover spaghetti, raining it onto the floor left and right like a bunch of skydiving earthworms.

"Charming *and* tidy," said Parker. "You're the perfect catch."

Boof glanced up, his lips, chin, and cheeks smeared red with tomato sauce. "Huh?"

"You're making a mess."

Just then, Parker's belly rumbled like an eighteen-wheeler crossing a bridge. He hadn't been able to force down more than a mouthful of dry dog food that morning, and he found he was starving now. The spilled spaghetti called to him like a siren's song.

But before Parker could succumb to eating off that filthy floor, Boof had spotted the dropped noodles, knelt down, and slurped them up. "There. All clean."

Parker winced. Seeing your own tongue licking the floor was super-gross. "Ugh. At least put some on a plate for me."

"Here." Boof set the Tupperware bowl on the floor and straightened, thrusting his head back into the open fridge. "Ooh, cheese!"

Parker hesitated. Was he really going to eat straight out of a Tupperware?

But the longer he stood there, the more delicious the

spaghetti smelled. Before he knew it, Parker had thrust his snout into the bowl and was gobbling up the contents with gusto. His tail curled under. Eating like a wild beast, without fork and spoon, without even hands was bad enough. But worse, some part of him really *enjoyed* gorging himself this way.

*That* was truly embarrassing.

Boof bit into a cheese wedge like a candy bar. "Now you're getting it," he mumbled around a mouthful of cheddar.

*That's what I'm afraid of,* thought Parker, licking up the last of the tomato sauce. Still, he couldn't deny how much fun it was to let his appetite run wild, like Boof did. No worries, no consequences. This feeling only intensified when Boof tossed him a chicken breast from his pile.

*Pig out!*

Toting an impressively random selection of eats—everything from raw eggs and carrots to leftover Thai food and apple pie—over to the table, Boof tore into it with a vengeance. Between bites of chicken, Parker watched, fascinated.

"Wow," he said.

"It's a gift," Boof mumbled through a mouthful of pie.

"When you finish your . . . snack," said Parker, "I need your help."

"With what?" Boof popped an egg into his mouth and bit down. Yellow yolk dribbled off his chin, and he spat the shell fragments onto the floor. "Mmm, crunchy."

"Eeeww." Okay, that was a little over the top. "Look," said Parker, "I can't use the computer with these paws. We've got to research how to fix our situation."

Boof turned an incredulous expression on him. "Fix it?" he said. "I'm living the dream."

"But I'm *not*," Parker whined. Strange, but he was almost getting used to barking and whining his words. "Come on, help me. This is your fault as much as mine."

Though Boof looked sympathetic, he only said, "Okay, yeah."

As Boof continued chowing down, Parker padded over to the stove, pulled a tea towel off the handle with his teeth, and draped it over Boof's mess. More food fragments rained down. Planting a paw on the towel, he began wiping it around, trying to clean up. It was a losing battle.

In a surprisingly brief time, Boof had scarfed down everything on the tabletop. He grinned, leaned back in his chair, and let out a supersonic burp.

"Now *that* was a snack," he said.

While pushing the towel over the last bits of eggshell,

Parker paused. How the heck was he going to scoop up all the food fragments and dump them in the trash, using only paws and a mouth?

He glanced up. "A little help here?"

Boof waved a hand. "Forget that. We need to play and make you happy. Time for fun!"

"After we clean up," said Parker.

Jumping to his feet, Boof said, "I know, let's go to the park!"

"But the mess," said Parker. "My computer search."

"Later." Boof grinned wider. "Fun first!" And with that, he rushed out of the kitchen and down the hall.

Glancing around at the snack catastrophe, Parker wavered. But when Boof yelled, "Woo-hoo! Park, park, park!" he knew he couldn't let this dog in human form go out into the world alone. It wasn't fair—to the world, to Boof, or to Parker's poor body.

Who knew what kind of trouble Boof would unleash?

Abandoning his cleanup, Parker loped down the hall in pursuit.

⇧⇩

Three long blocks away from the Pitts' home, the city park erupted from the surrounding suburbs like a Mohawk on a bald man's dome. Its wild tangle of greenery bristled with broad shade trees and here and there a stretch of well-tended lawn. In one fenced-off corner, dog owners let their pets run off-leash while they gossiped.

Parker had been here once or twice before with Billie and Boof.

But never as a dog.

The closer they came to the park, the slower Parker's steps grew. He could see as well as smell the dogs there—a miniature pinscher, a couple of pit bulls, a golden retriever, a Great Dane, a handful of mutts, and an enormous hairy thing he'd never learned the breed of—and he had no interest in meeting them. They'd probably gang up on him once they smelled that he was a fake. They'd probably bite him and give him rabies, then he'd get sick and die.

Or a fate even worse.

Parker looked around for something to clean.

Pausing with one hand on the gate, Boof glanced over at him. "Let's do it."

Parker sat. "You go ahead. I'll watch."

"See, this is your whole problem." Boof strode over and grabbed Parker's collar. "You never have any fun."

"Sure I do." Parker felt indignation rising like hot steam from a volcanic vent. "I have fun all the time."

*Don't I?*

Boof tugged on the collar. "Watching the picture box with your mother and father doesn't count."

Digging in his heels, Parker said, "I make things tidy. I organize. I read."

"*Pfft!* Whatever that stuff is, it doesn't count either." Step by step, Boof muscled him over to the gate.

"Hey, stop dragging me!"

"What, and let you miss out?" said Boof.

"Just because I don't want a bunch of strange dogs smelling my butt doesn't mean I don't enjoy life," said Parker.

"You don't get it." Boof unlatched the gate.

"I don't want to."

Shaking his head, Boof said, "See, this is what it's all about. You gotta run around, sniff things, get muddy, eat something mysterious."

"Like raccoon poop? No, thanks."

"Life is supposed to be *fun*." Shoving Parker through the fence, Boof cried, "Let's play!"

A couple of older women standing nearby chuckled. "Aw, the poor woofer," said one of them. "He's feeling shy."

"I'm not shy!" Parker barked at them. "And I'm not a dog!"

"Here, poochie." The taller woman bent down, extending her hand with knuckles forward.

Ignoring her, Parker spun around and made straight

for the gate. But Boof blocked him. "Come on. You want to be a Good Dog, don't you?"

"I don't want to be a dog at—*Ah!*" Parker jumped. Someone had jammed a cold, wet nose into his unprotected butt. When he turned, the Great Dane was looming over him, as big as a house.

"Hello," she rumbled.

"Heh. Nice doggie," said Parker. He could feel his tail tucking under, and he backed into the fence.

"Now it's your turn," said Boof. "Go ahead, sniff her."

"You sniff her," said Parker.

To his surprise, Boof squatted down, stuck his nose under the Dane's tail, and took a deep whiff.

The tall woman raised a hand to her mouth in horror.

"Stupid human nose," said Boof. "I can barely smell what she had for breakfast."

Parker's lip curled. "Why would you want to?"

Straightening up, Boof said, "It's what we do. Now your turn."

"But I—"

"Don't be rude," said Boof.

Parker gazed up at the enormous, jowly dog with its tail curled into dominant position. Maybe you shouldn't tick off something that could eat you as a snack? Gingerly, he stepped forward and took a whiff.

"Aw, isn't it cute how he's coaching his dog?" said the shorter woman to her friend. The taller dog owner sent Boof a doubtful look.

He grinned at them. "He's sweet, but kinda slow."

Parker would have objected, but his senses were swamped by all the information flooding into his brain through the Great Dane's scent. He could tell that she was young, that her dog food had chicken in it, that she was happy but nervous, that she lived with a cat, and that she was about to come into heat.

His jaw dropped. Amazing.

"So, is she?" asked Boof. "In heat, I mean. I can't quite tell with this nose."

Parker just nodded.

The Dane wagged, and Parker felt his own tail wagging in response. She gave a joyful *woof* that registered as "Let's play!" Then, in a flash, she made a puppy bow—chest low, rear end high—and scampered away, looking back at them.

"Let's chase her," said Boof. "Come on!" And with a whoop, he took off after the Great Dane.

*Well, why not?* thought Parker.

And at that thought, his body leaped into action. He felt strong; he felt agile. This dog body had so much energy, he didn't know what to do with it.

So he ran.

The Dane led them a merry chase, up the gentle slope and back down again, blasting past the pit bulls and mutts. Boof whooped again, and Parker released a string of happy barks. A sense of wonder swept over him. This was . . . *fun.* Parker felt like a weight had lifted off his shoulders.

And then, as suddenly as it had begun, the game ended. The Great Dane caught an intriguing scent from a bush and stopped on a dime to investigate. Boof and Parker stumbled to a halt.

"Whew!" said Boof.

"I *liked* that!" said Parker.

He caught his breath. The running had felt *good.* No wonder Boof caused so much trouble when he hadn't been walked—too much pent-up energy. Parker felt a flash of sympathy for the dog who had taken over his body.

It didn't last long.

"Now, what we really need is . . ." Scanning the park, Boof spotted the golden retriever loping toward them, chasing a tennis ball his owner had thrown. Before the dog could reach it, Boof darted over and scooped the ball off the grass. "Ha-ha! I've got your ball," he taunted in a singsong tone.

"Don't steal his—" called Parker. But Boof danced

away, holding his prize high as the retriever pursued, leaping after it.

Parker edged a few steps closer. The dog's bark had a sharp edge to it—saying, "Give it! Give it!"—and Parker could smell his frustration from ten feet away.

"Give him back the ball," Parker said.

Instead, Boof dangled it just out of reach. "Oh, this? You want this? I don't have it." And he chucked the ball to Parker, who without thinking reared up and caught it in his mouth.

The golden retriever wheeled on him with a savage glare.

*Uh-oh.*

Parker turned and fled. After a few steps, he glanced back and saw the other dog in hot pursuit. A mustard-furred mutt raised its head. Drawn to the fuss, it quickly joined the chase.

"Go, Boy, go!" cried Boof, trailing behind them.

Hot adrenaline coursed through Parker's body like a lava milkshake. This wasn't fun anymore. The golden was drawing closer and closer, and the mutt trotted just behind him.

Why wouldn't these dogs leave him alone?

In a flash, Parker realized he still carried the stupid ball in his mouth. He spat it out and ducked around behind a tree trunk.

But the retriever dodged the other way. He loomed before Parker, legs braced and fangs bared.

"My ball!" he snarled.

Skidding to a stop, Parker yelped, "I don't have it."

The dog's eyes narrowed to slits. "I don't care."

# PARKER ⇨

# 8

# Dogfight

Parker was a dead man—or a dead dog—and he knew it. The golden retriever was not that much bigger than him, but he was a whole lot angrier and probably knew how to fight. Parker backed up, eyes glued to his adversary.

"Take back your ball," he said. "It's over by that bush."

The dog just growled and kept advancing.

Parker glanced at the mustard-colored mutt, who was absorbed in the action. "Tell him. There's no need for violence."

"Fight! Fight! Fight!" barked the mutt.

"So helpful," said Parker. All the hair on his shoulders stood up, and his legs went stiff.

Boof finally caught up to the dogs. "Whatever you do, don't show weakness," he told Parker. "Don't act scared."

"But I *am* scared," said Parker.

The retriever growled. "You should be."

Circling around Parker, the other dog peeled back his lip to reveal loads of sharp white teeth.

Parker circled the other way. "Can't we just talk this out?" Where was the dog's owner? Off getting a pumpkin spice latte?

In a sudden blond blur, the retriever lunged, snarling like a wampa monster craving a Skywalker snack. Instinct took over, and Parker snarled back.

*Whomp!* The two dogs collided. As the retriever wrapped its front paws around his neck, Parker surged upward, breaking the hold.

A hot pain scored his ear. *Yipe!* That stinker had bitten him!

Red rage torched Parker's fear. He whacked the retriever's nose with his paw, hard as he could, and was rewarded with a yelp from the other dog.

"Leave it!" a woman bellowed. And the next thing Parker knew, a stocky brunette had waded into the fight, seizing the retriever by his collar.

"Let me at him!" barked the dog. But the woman hauled him away, apologizing to Boof as she went.

"Yeah, you *better* run," said Parker weakly. Now that the fight was over, his legs felt wobblier than a kindergartner's Popsicle-stick house. He hung his head, sucking in gulps of sweet air.

*That was a close one.*

"Give it a shake," said Boof, joining him.

"What?"

"Your body." Boof demonstrated by shaking himself all over. "It always makes me feel better."

Parker shot him a doubtful look. But he followed the advice, his ears *whap-whap-whapping* against his cheeks. Afterward, not only did the hair on his shoulders lie back down, but Parker actually felt calmer.

*Huh. Who knew?*

"So you had your first fight," said Boof. "Good for you."

Now that the adrenaline was ebbing, Parker noticed a dull throb from the ear the other dog had bitten. "What's so good about fighting? It's scary and messy, and it hurts."

Boof shrugged. "Exactly. Pretty great, yeah?"

Parker shook his head. Sometimes it felt like he and Boof were speaking two different languages. "My parents always say that if you resort to fighting, you've already lost the argument."

"Huh?" Boof frowned, cocking his head. "Fighting is part of life. Sometimes you've got to fight for what you want. Or defend yourself if someone attacks."

All Parker wanted right then was to drink a lake's worth of water, lie down, and get his ear disinfected. In fact, now that he thought about it, who knew where that other dog's mouth had been? Who knew what kind of germs were dog-paddling through Parker's bloodstream at this very moment?

His skin prickled. "Can we go home?"

With a last longing look at the other dogs romping and playing, Boof sighed. "Oh, I guess. You've had enough fun for now."

⇧⇩

Boof and Parker were on their own for dinner. Over the past months, Parker had gotten used to this—sometimes he and Billie had taken turns making meals after their grandma passed—but his new body was not built for cooking. Try as Parker might, he wasn't about to become the world's first doggie chef. And that meant a repeat of Boof's snack extravaganza for both their dinners.

It was a muddle, but it wasn't bad.

Later, Mom and Dad returned home with dessert and were somewhat less than pleased with the chaos in the kitchen. Parker had to lie there by the table and listen to his parents scold him (well, Boof, actually) for being such a slob.

"You've been so helpful the past few months," said his mother. "How could you leave such a mess today?"

Boof lifted a shoulder. "It was easy."

"Don't sass your mother, little man." Parker's dad pointed at Boof with a cake-laden fork. "She works hard all day. She doesn't need more stress when she comes home."

"Your bed wasn't made, your book bag was lying in the middle of the hallway, and this kitchen was a disaster area," said Parker's mom. "Honey, you know better than that."

Parker sank his chin on his paws. "Told you so," he muttered.

Boof looked from one adult to the other, mystified. "I don't get it. What's so important about cleaning up?"

Parker's parents gaped. "Excuse me, is this the same son I've been living with all these years?" said his mom. "What did you do to Parker?"

At that, Parker and Boof exchanged a glance.

His dad scowled. "So you've changed. I suppose now you'd rather live in a pigsty?"

"That depends." Boof considered the question. "Do pigs eat Pup-Peroni?"

"Boof!" said Parker.

Parker's father rumbled, "That's it. No more dessert for you." He slid Boof's slice of cake away from him.

Oblivious to the man's scolding, Boof said, "What? I didn't know the pigsty was an option."

"Go," said Parker's dad. "Clean up your room. Think about what you've done."

Boof slouched. It really seemed to bother him when people were unhappy. "But I don't—"

"Enough," said Parker, tugging on his pants leg. "Let's go."

Observing this, his mom said, "Look, even the dog wants you to mend your ways."

Boof rose from the table and nearly left the room without carrying his plate to the sink. A few words from Parker's mom fixed that. But when they reached the stairs, Parker blocked Boof's way.

"What now?" Boof whined.

"You made me a promise, Mr. Slob."

Boof frowned. "I did?"

"Yup. Before we go upstairs, you and I are doing that computer research," said Parker.

Boof blinked. "I have no idea what you just said."

"I'll show you. Come."

In the family room, the desktop computer rested in sleep mode. Images of Billie onstage, family vacations, and embarrassing school photos floated across the screen. At a shot of Grandma Mimi surfing the North Shore of Oahu, Parker winced. She'd looked so happy and full of life then, but now . . .

He gulped. *Don't think about it*, he ordered himself, fighting the urge to straighten the couch cushions.

"Okay," said Parker. "Sit down in the chair and click on the mouse."

"Mouse? Where?" Boof scanned the room eagerly.

"Not a real mouse," said Parker. "Sit."

Boof sat.

"Hey, why are they so mad?" he asked. "Don't they like me?"

"My parents?" Parker frowned. Could Boof really be that dense? "Of course they like you—me. But you made a really big mess and didn't clean it up."

Boof nodded. "Right. So?"

Blowing out a sigh, Parker said, as if to a first grader, "So *they* had to clean it up for you, and they didn't like that."

Boof kept nodding, his brow furrowed. "I'm not following you."

"You're not taking responsibility," said Parker.

"Respon-si . . . bility?" Boof pronounced the word as if it was some disgusting new vegetable on the menu.

"Yeah, it means you do what's expected of you and take the consequences when you fail."

"Riiight," said Boof. From his expression, he hadn't understood a word.

Parker snapped, "Boof, your actions affect other people, okay?"

"Okay . . ."

Parker closed his eyes. How do you explain responsibility to a dog? It was like explaining break dancing to an inchworm.

"Look, never mind—just push that oblong white thing by the keyboard." Parker pointed his nose at the computer mouse. When Boof complied and the computer woke up, Parker said, "Now move the mouse with your hand."

Boof chuckled. "It's got no tail. Some mouse."

"See how that arrow goes across the screen when you push the mouse? Shift it over that blue circle and press down once."

"Squish the mousie!" said Boof, delighted with himself. The web browser opened a new window.

"Whatever," said Parker. "Now move the arrow into that long white bubble at the top."

"This one?"

"Press down again. Now type 'how to switch souls.' "

Boof looked at the screen; he looked at Parker. He frowned. "Type?"

"Oh, boy."

This was going to take a while.

After Parker painstakingly directed Boof to punch in

each letter and eventually hit enter, they clicked through the search results. An ad from a psychic medium. An ad from a New Agey store in town. (Mimi would've loved that.) An article on soul swapping in the movies. A blog post about something called "walk-ins," which sported phrases like "karmic matrix" and "the advanced soul's greater enlightenment."

The concepts were confusing enough. Compound that with a headache from trying to read with doggie eyes, and Parker could barely continue. Then he spotted something, and his heart sank like a brick in a fish tank. "Ugh."

"What?"

"This website says the switch is permanent," said Parker.

"Hmm?" Bored with the internet, Boof was batting the mouse around on the tabletop like a cat with a toy. He clicked on a link to a different website. "Oops."

"Stop messing around," said Parker. "This is serious. If we can't find a cure, I'll be eating Alpo for the rest of my life."

"And what's wrong with that?" Boof swiveled back and forth in the chair, and then with a push, he lifted his feet and spun all the way around. "Wheee!"

"Enough!" barked Parker.

Then he happened to read the page Boof had clicked on,

something called LearningSpells.com, and his jaw dropped. There it was, under a cartoon of a witch with hands raised: *Spell Casting Instructions for Body Switch.* Through his throbbing headache, he scanned the lines. Could it be that simple? Could solving his problem be as easy as reading an incantation?

Mimi would've loved this "woo-woo stuff," as she called it. Parker's eyes misted at the thought. They'd had long discussions about whether magic was real, where it could be found, and how it might operate. Ironic that she'd missed the greatest magic ever to affect Parker's life.

While Parker read, Boof wandered over to the bookshelf to play with his dad's collection of bobblehead dolls. "Hey, they bounce!"

Parker ignored him, focusing on the screen. The instructions said to concentrate on the person you wanted to swap bodies with, and repeat the lines of the spell, first in your head and then aloud. He sat up and read through it silently, then spoke the words:

*"Gods and goddesses, hear my plea*
*And help me switch to my true body."*

Boof glanced over at him. "Huh?"

Undeterred, Parker continued the chant.

*"Boof's is the body I need to swap,*
*It'll happen fast, with a little pop.*
*No pain, no hurt, no sharp surprise,*
*I'll see the world through different eyes.*
*Please grant my wish and make it be,*
*That I be him, and he be me!"*

Boof wrinkled his nose. "Really? That's it?"

"According to whoever wrote this," said Parker. He stared at Boof. Boof stared back. "Feel any different?"

Boof belched. "No. But I'm not sure I like beans."

Gazing down at his doggie body, Parker tried to sense any tingles or changes happening inside. Nothing. Except maybe something that felt like a flea on his shoulder. He rubbed it against a table leg.

"Maybe it'll happen in our sleep," said Parker. "Like last time."

Footsteps clattered in the hallway. "Honey, how's that room cleaning coming along?" Parker's mom called up the stairs.

Out of habit, Parker began to answer her, then caught himself. "Tell her we're down here and you're finishing your homework," he said.

"Just doing my homework, Mom," said Boof.

Parker's mother appeared in the doorway. "Oh. Well,

wrap it up now and tackle that room, then maybe you can watch some videos before bedtime."

"Videos?" Boof's expression was as blank as an essay on *Why I love doing homework over summer vacation.* "What's that?"

Parker's mom chuckled. "Funny guy." She took a step into the room, peering at the screen. "What are you working on?"

A fluttery feeling swept through Parker's belly. He couldn't let his mom see the website. While Boof stammered some answer, Parker reared up on his hind legs and swatted at the keyboard's power button with a paw.

The computer shut down the browser, and the screen slowly went black. His mom stared at Parker. "Did . . . did the dog just turn that off?"

*Whoops.*

Flopping down onto his side, Parker scratched himself, trying to look as doggish as possible. He flinched when he accidentally scratched his wounded ear.

"I, uh . . ." Boof chewed his lip. "I'm teaching him a new trick."

"A trick?" she asked.

"Yeah, to use the, um . . ." Boof gestured at the desktop.

"Computer?" Parker's mom snorted a laugh. "You've

got your work cut out for you. While you're at it, try teaching him something useful, like how to cook eggs Benedict."

"Okay," said Boof. "If you think it would help."

Parker's mom chuckled, ruffling Boof's hair. "It's nice that you're making an effort with him. See? Boof's not so bad after all."

"Bad?" said Boof. "He's the best dog ever."

Parker rolled his eyes.

His mother gave Boof a gentle push. "Now, get up there. The sooner you finish, the sooner you can play."

Boy and dog padded up the stairs together. "And the sooner we get to sleep," said Parker, "the sooner we can wake up in our own bodies, back to normal."

"You think so?" asked Boof.

Parker grinned a doggie grin. "Trust me. Tomorrow, this whole long nightmare will be just a memory."

⇦BOOF

# 9

# The Biter

When the alarm clock rang, Boof stretched luxuriously, extending his arms and legs to their fullest reach. Then he rolled over and pressed that button on the noisy machine like Parker had shown him, and the beeping stopped.

He smiled. He was really getting the hang of this "being a human" stuff.

"Noooo!" came a wail from the floor beside the bed.

Boof glanced over to see Parker lift his head from his paws and examine them in horror. "It didn't work! I'm still a dog."

"And I'm still awesome," said Boof, trying to cheer him up. "Let's go eat!"

Parker moaned and dragged along behind as Boof marked his territory in the bathroom, scolding him with some nonsense about washing his hands or improving his aim. Boof hated to see him upset, but sometimes he just tuned Gloomy Boy out. It was easier that way.

Downstairs, Flower Woman introduced him to cereal with berries. That was . . . interesting. Boof didn't like it as much as the pig strips he'd eaten the day before, but really, almost all food was good food, and his human mouth really loved something about the cereal.

"I still can't believe that's not too sugary for you," said the woman.

*Sugary.* Maybe that was the taste? "I like it," said Boof through a mouthful of cereal.

Parker bopped him with a paw. "Chew with your mouth closed," he said. "You're dripping milk."

Suffering cats, that kid could suck all the joy out of the simplest things.

Boof still couldn't get over the amount and variety of food available to him. After polishing off the cereal and stuffing his face with something called *muffins*, Boof was ready to visit the cold white box to see what else was on offer. But Flower Woman had other plans.

She handed him some small pieces of paper and metal, just like yesterday, and said, "For lunch," and then hustled him upstairs to get ready for school.

Unlike Parker's distracted father the day before, she made sure he took a stand-up bath under this spout thingy that sprayed water all over him. (Parker told him how to work it.) Afterward, Boof shook himself all over to sluice off the water, until the Boy made him use a towel.

What was the point of the stand-up bath? Boof didn't understand. He was just going to get dirty all over again, and besides, the water washed off all the wonderful smells he'd accumulated the day before.

This time, Flower Woman drove him to school, leaving Parker behind to stare after them with a mournful expression. This troubled Boof. As he hung his head out the car window, he wondered what the problem was. Maybe the Boy wasn't appreciating just how cool it was to be a dog? After school, he'd have to coach Gloomy Boy.

When the car stopped in front of the school, Parker's mother put a hand on Boof's shoulder and kissed him on the cheek. "Have a great day," she said.

Boof grinned. "I always do."

She tilted her head. "There's something different about you."

"Oh?" Boof thought he'd been doing a pretty good job pretending to be Parker.

"That's the first time since school started that you've let me kiss you goodbye at drop-off," said the woman.

"Um . . ." Boof didn't know what to say.

"I like it." The Boy's mother patted his cheek. "Now, hurry up and don't be late."

Once again, Boof marveled at the river of humans flowing from the cars and buses through the gate. What drew them back here day after day? It wasn't the food. He'd eaten it yesterday, and the food was much better at home. It wasn't the playtime. A half hour of exercise? Barely adequate.

He shrugged. Who could understand humans?

Just like the day before, he bumped into pug-faced Cody in the main hall.

"Dude!" the boy greeted him. "How's your head?"

"My head?"

"Yeah, you know . . ." Cody rapped his knuckles on his own forehead. "The memory loss? All that?"

"Oh. Yeah." It was hard to keep all the stories straight. Boof wondered how Parker managed. "Um . . . about the same."

Punching his arm, the boy said, "Stick with me like a grommet on a longboard. I'll get you through this." Boof was learning more and more human talk, but sometimes it seemed Cody was speaking Cat.

As they strolled down the hall, Cody went on about his "show" (whatever that was) and how totally radical it had been last night.

Somehow, Boof sensed that all Cody needed from him were nods and "uh-huh"s, so he kept them coming. Then they rounded a corner and Cody stopped in his tracks.

"What?" asked Boof.

From the side of his mouth, Cody muttered something that sounded like "Deke the Freak," though Boof couldn't be sure.

"Huh?" he asked.

But Cody fell silent as a huge boy with the look of a Rottweiler lumbered toward them. Taking a cue from his friend, Boof went on alert. Without his former keen nose or the clear visual cues that strange dogs provided, Boof had a hard time reading this new boy. He looked closer.

Rottweiler Boy was smiling a little, but not with his eyes. And the set of his shoulders hinted that maybe this visit wasn't a friendly one. Boof stiffened, as he would when meeting any strange mutt.

"Hey, hobbits," said the new boy.

"Hey, Deke," Cody said to the floor.

"My name isn't Hobbit, it's Boo—um, Parker," said Boof. He shifted his stance, giving himself room to move if needed.

"Well, hello, Booum Parker." Deke sneered. "Why don't you hand over that lunch money?"

"I don't know," said Boof. "Why don't I?"

Cody gasped.

Rottweiler Boy opened his palm in front of Boof's chest. "Because I want it, that's why."

"Want what?" asked Boof.

"Your lunch money, dweezil." Deke's eyebrows drew together, and aggressive energy radiated from him like heat from a roaring fireplace.

"I don't know what that is," said Boof. Usually people liked him, but something was off about this new kid. The little hairs on his neck rose. Boof shifted his weight onto the balls of his feet, watching Deke's eyes.

"Oh, yeah?" said Rottweiler Boy. One meaty hand shot out and gripped Boof's shoulder. The other clenched into a fist. "How about I refresh your—*Agh!*"

Reacting on instinct, Boof had twisted his head and bitten the hand on his shoulder.

Deke scuttled back, cradling his wounded paw. His eyes were wide, and his voice squeaked. "You . . . bit me."

"Yup," said Boof.

"Wi-with your teeth," Rottweiler Boy sputtered.

"Uh-huh."

A ring of kids formed around them, watching the action. They looked happy, excited.

"And if you try that again, I'll bite your other hand," said Boof. Now that he knew this was a simple dominance challenge, he felt he was on familiar ground.

Several kids in the circle said, "Ooh." Again, Deke was hard to read, his expression somewhere between fear, wonder, and rage.

Still watching the big boy, Boof asked Cody, "Don't we have somewhere to be?"

"Oh, yeah. Cowabunga!" Cody beamed a sudden smile, looped his arm through Boof's, and started off.

Side-eyeing Rottweiler Boy, Boof stalked past him, through the ring of kids and down the corridor. On the way, several of them patted his shoulder or tried to bump his fist with theirs.

"Way to go," said a skinny boy.

"Wow!" said a redheaded girl. "Just . . . wow."

Cody was staring at Boof with his mouth open. The silence stretched as they walked on.

"What?" asked Boof at last.

"You're either totally bazonkers or you're my hero."

"I am?" Boof raised his eyebrows. "Why?"

Wordless, Cody gestured from Boof to Deke and the kids up the hall. Then he frowned at a sudden thought. "Tell me something."

"What's that?"

"Exactly how hard did you hit your head?"

⇧⇩

All through that day, Boof tried to remember Parker's warning about not causing trouble, and he made an effort to be a Good Dog—er, Boy. But how was he supposed to know that it wasn't okay to mark your territory on the bushes by the cafeteria? Or leave the classroom when you felt restless?

Nobody warned him not to do these things, but somehow all the other kids seemed to magically know the right behavior already. Did it have something to do with those little black marks on paper that everyone seemed so keen on?

Boof had no clue.

After the second time he'd put his head down and fallen asleep on his desktop, Mrs. Scales shook him awake.

"Is my teaching interfering with your nap time?" asked the woman with the bulldog face.

Blinking and yawning, Boof said, "No, it actually helps me sleep."

Cody snorted, stifling a laugh. Some of the other kids chuckled.

Seen from up close, Mrs. Scales's face was caked with some light brown powdery substance, and her eyes looked wearier than that old dog down the street with the white-furred muzzle. When she sighed, a smell like cabbage and stuffy closets drifted over Boof.

"Since you seem determined not to learn anything today, why don't you go to Principal Anidi's office?" she said. "Maybe she can figure out what to do with you."

"Okay," said Boof, visions of cookies dancing in his head. He rose and made to leave, but the teacher held up a hand. "Wait. I'm sending a note with you."

As Mrs. Scales trudged back to her desk and fished a pink pad from her drawer, that nice-smelling Gabi girl smiled, beckoning Boof to join her. He padded over to the girl's desk.

"I never knew you were such a bad boy," she said in a teasing tone.

Boof shrugged. "I try to be good. Things happen."

When Gabi smiled, little divots appeared in her cheeks. She lowered her voice. "Why don't you come over after school today and play? We could have some fun."

Boof brightened. "I like fun."

As she slipped him a scrap of paper with some black marks on it, she said, "Here's my number. Meet me by the flagpole after school, and we can ride with my mom."

A raspy voice distracted him. "Mr. Pitts, did I ask you to talk with Miss Cortez?" the teacher asked.

"No, she did." Boof pointed at Gabi.

With a long-suffering look, Mrs. Scales held up a pink slip of paper. "Take this to the office. Please."

Nodding to Gabi, Boof ambled down the aisle to the teacher's desk and collected the paper. He waited a moment, in case the woman wanted to give him a treat or praise. None was forthcoming.

"Sometime this century," said Mrs. Scales.

Boof raised his eyebrows in a question.

"Go. Now."

What else could Boof do? He went.

# PARKER ⇨

# 10

# Hole New Thing

Parker growled. This was maddening. Here he was, stuck in this doggie body for a second day, with no one to talk to but Boof. The food was disgusting. Relieving himself outdoors was gross. And it seemed like he was always scratching himself, because of the fleas or mites or whatever that crawled all over him.

Heck, earlier this morning it had gotten so bad, he'd run himself a bath with his clumsy dog paws and soaked until he thought he'd drowned the bugs. Of course, cleaning all the dog hair out of the tub afterward was a nightmare. He'd had to drop a towel in there to mop everything up, and he couldn't use Comet to make things sparkle.

Parker just knew his mom wouldn't be thrilled.

And now, here it was, lunchtime. But instead of enjoying a nice, boring school lunch with Cody, he was trying to break into the fridge without hands. The refrigerator door had a powerful seal, which was resisting all his efforts to pry it open.

It was like trying to pick a lock with a limp sardine.

Frustrated, he padded over to the pantry door, nosed it open, and inhaled the rich variety of food smells. Ah, this was more like it. Parker reared up, planting his front paws on the highest shelf he could reach. He scanned around for a snack.

Uncooked pasta? Nope. A jar of pickles? Nah.

Peanut butter! He started to reach for the jar, then realized it would be impossible for him to unscrew the lid.

Parker growled again. Being a dog sucked.

When he lifted a box of Frosted Flakes off the shelf with his teeth and set it down on the tiles, he paused. Exactly how was he supposed to eat this? Stick his snout in and munch it from the box? Or spill it and wolf the flakes off the floor?

At the thought, his stomach rolled. What if he caught some disease off the filthy tiles and died like Mimi? What if that little bit of chaos led to more chaos, and his whole world fell apart? Worse than it had already? Parker shuddered all over.

To calm his mind, he spent a few minutes organizing the items on the lower shelves until they were all labels-out. But finally, his hunger wouldn't be denied. Parker ended up taking a can of cashews from a low shelf, prying off the plastic top with his teeth, and pouring cashews onto the lid before eating. It wasn't the best solution, but it helped satisfy the rumble in his belly.

Restless, Parker roamed the house. His paws were too clumsy to work the computer on his own (he'd tried), and nobody would be home for hours. He thought about visiting the New Age store for help (Mimi would've approved), but he doubted they'd understand doggie sign language. He'd need Boof along to talk to the store owner.

What to do?

As Parker padded through the family room, he passed by Mimi's chair and caught a strong whiff of her sandalwood perfume. The scent penetrated straight to his brain. Unbidden, a memory arose.

He'd been eight or nine, just back from kickboxing class, sniffling about some older kid's insult. Mimi had wrapped him in a warm hug that smelled of lemon bars and her perfume. Then she sat him down on the couch beside her and listened to his troubles.

"Jason called me a bad word," he'd said. "He told me the brown would never wash off my skin, that I'd always be ugly."

"Hush," she'd said, drying his tears. "That fool doesn't know what he's blabbing about." Mimi had told him that brown was beautiful, that his skin was a gift from his ancestors on both sides of the family, and that ugly came from the inside, not the outside.

"He's just jealous 'cause you're so pretty and he's not," she'd said, giving him a squeeze.

Within minutes, he was laughing again, spraying bits of lemon bar onto the carpet. Mimi always had a magical ability to change his mood.

Parker glanced down at the rug, half expecting to see lemon bar crumbs. A sense of loss hit him like a gut punch, followed by an intense urge to clean. But again, this doggie body limited him. Parker could do no more than fluff up the pillows and shelve a misplaced book.

It wasn't enough.

The compulsion kept building. He didn't know what to do with it. Driven to move, Parker trotted into the kitchen, through the doggie door, and out into the backyard. The cool breeze stirred his fur and the sunshine warmed him, but that didn't help.

What would? Mimi alive again, back in his life, loving and guiding him and understanding him like no one else. She'd always been there for Parker, much more than his parents or sister had. Heck, she'd probably even figure out a way to reverse this stupid soul switch.

In his gut and throat, the pressure grew and grew,

becoming almost unbearable. When he could take it no more, Parker sat down, threw his head back, and howled.

It just. Wasn't. Fair.

Three or four good howls later, he felt a teensy bit better. Parker was drawing breath for another round, when a gruff growl reached his ears.

"Put a sock in it, will ya? I'm trying to sleep over here."

Scanning the yard, Parker saw no one. He sniffed the air. "Hello?"

"Follow my voice." The bark seemed to be coming from behind the wooden fence, and by the sound of it, the dog was a big one.

Drawing closer, Parker said, "I—sorry, I didn't mean . . ."

"Relax, kid," said the other dog. "I'm not gonna bite ya."

Putting his nose to a gap between the planks, Parker took a deep whiff. Someone sniffed back. His doggie senses told him that the neighbor dog was female and older than him, and he pictured the Johnsons' pet. Was her name Roxy? Lulu?

"Rough day?" asked the older dog.

"I—yeah," said Parker. "I'm just plain miserable."

"Well, try being silently miserable."

Parker turned away. "So sorry if my wretched life disturbed you."

"Aw, don't be that way," said the older dog. "I'm cranky when I first wake up, that's all."

Parker felt funny talking to someone he couldn't see. "Um, what's your name again?"

"They call me Ruby," said the dog. "And you're Boof, right?"

"Uh, not exactly."

"How's that?"

And Parker squatted by the fence, pouring out his tale of woe, from the ruined farewell party, to the failed spell, to his current predicament. The older dog listened patiently, not interrupting once.

When he'd finished, she said, "Tell me one thing."

"Okay."

"Are ya nuts?"

*"No!"* wailed Parker. "I'm stuck in this stupid doggie body and it's *driving* me nuts."

"Okay, okay," said Ruby. "Enough howling. It's just—ya know your story sounds bonkers, right?"

"I know," said Parker. "Believe me."

Ruby was silent for a few heartbeats. Parker stood, figuring that was that.

"Ya sound kinda down in the dumps," she said.

"Not me," said Parker. "I'm jumping for joy."

"Ah, sarcasm." Ruby scratched herself so loudly he

could hear it from the other side of the fence. "Have ya tried rubbing your butt against a tree?"

"No."

"How about chewing up a nice stinky pair of dirty underwear?"

"Eew, no!" Parker's lip curled.

"Eating from a cat's litter box?"

"Oh, come on," said Parker. "That's disgusting."

He could almost hear her shrug. "Don't knock it till you've tried it."

Parker turned to go. "Thanks anyway."

"Ya know what your problem is?" said the older dog.

He scoffed. "Uh, yeah. Slightly."

"You're not enjoying being a dog."

Even though Ruby couldn't see him, Parker couldn't help rolling his eyes. "Well, duh. Why would I?"

"No, listen, kiddo. I know ya wanna get back to your own body. I get it. But until ya do, you're stuck with the one you're in."

Knocking his forehead against the fence, Parker said, "Tell me something I don't know."

"That's why ya need to enjoy it," she said.

"Huh?"

"You—" Ruby broke off. "This isn't working, not seeing ya. How are ya at digging?"

The sudden change of subject threw Parker. "Excuse me?"

Scratching the fence with her claws, Ruby said, "Dig here. I'll dig from this side."

"*This* is how I enjoy being a dog?"

"No, genius. When the hole gets deep enough, you visit me."

Parker looked around his yard. Not exactly a hotbed of excitement. And it wasn't like he had anything better to do before Boof came home.

Despite his aversion to getting dirty, Parker started digging.

The ground was soft, and before five minutes had passed, they'd dug a hole deep enough to accommodate him. Parker wriggled under the fence and popped up in the Johnsons' backyard, a sprawling, overgrown garden with more nooks and crannies than an English muffin.

He shook himself all over, hoping to get rid of the dirt.

"That's the ticket," said a rough voice.

Standing beside the hole was a Great Pyrenees. *Great* didn't begin to describe it. The dog was roughly the size of the Death Star, covered in a forest's worth of shaggy white fur, with sharp coffee-colored eyes and a dirty nose.

"Ruby?" said Parker.

"Well, it ain't the Easter Bunny," said the older dog, coming around to sniff his butt.

Feeling dwarfed, Parker let her smell him. He'd seen the dog a couple of times before, back when he was in human form. But it was another thing altogether to have her looming over you.

"Now, when do your people come home?" asked Ruby. "When the sun goes behind the roofline?"

Eyeing the house, Parker said, "I guess?"

"Good. Come with me."

Parker balked. "Where are we going?"

Nudging him along with her big wet nose, Ruby said, "To discover just how much fun it is being a dog."

"Can't wait," said Parker with a sigh. "But I'm not eating any kitty litter."

PARKER ⇨

# 11

# The Joys of Dogginess

Ruby led the way, squeezing under a thick hedge that ran the width of the Johnsons' backyard. "They have no idea this is how I get out," said the older dog. "Suckers."

"Right," said Parker. He couldn't help noticing that she was leaving scraps of white fur on the twisted branches, a dead giveaway.

"Don't—*unh*—get me wrong." Ruby flattened herself, wriggling through a particularly dense patch. "I love my people. But sometimes, a dog's gotta get out on her own, see the world. Know what I mean?"

"Not exactly," said Parker.

"Ya will." Popping up from under the hedge, Ruby led the way along the alley that ran behind the houses. "Let's see what trouble we can stir up."

"Trouble?" For a moment, Parker's doggish side sparked to the sound of this. Then he thought twice. "Uh, that's not fun."

One side of Ruby's mouth quirked up. "Then you're doing it wrong."

With mixed feelings, Parker trailed the bigger dog. Just down the alley, they passed a couple of stinky trash cans waiting for the next day's pickup.

"Ah!" Ruby took a deep whiff. "Smell that?"

"A zombie with a head cold could smell that," said Parker.

Ramming her shoulder into the first can, Ruby knocked it over, spilling bags of trash onto the pavement. She clawed them open with powerful strokes of her forelegs. "Yeah! That's the real deal."

"Eewww, gross," said Parker. He found his doggie mouth was starting to drool over the spoiled food, which made matters even more disgusting.

"You're missing out." Rooting through the mess, the larger dog unearthed a T-bone with a smidgen of steak still on it. She made short work of the treat, then went down on her shoulder in the garbage.

"Fancy a roll?" she said.

"That's sick," said Parker. "That steak probably had maggots on it, and who knows what kind of germs you're covering your body with? To say nothing of the stink."

"That's kinda the point." Ruby climbed to her feet and gave a vigorous shake. "Kid, ya gotta loosen up."

Parker's mouth twisted. "That's what everyone says." He'd always been happy with how he was, keeping the world nice and orderly. But he was beginning to wonder if there was another way of being. A way that was more . . . fun?

Ruby grinned a doggie grin. "I got just the ticket." Lumbering along to the next intersection, she looked both ways.

"What are you doing?" asked Parker.

"Watching for the Bad Man."

Parker's mouth went dry and he scanned the street. "What Bad Man?"

"He drives around in a truck capturing dogs and cats," said Ruby.

"You mean the Animal Control guy?"

The older dog just growled in reply. "Coast is clear," she said. "Now, check this out." Stalking as stealthily as a hundred-pound dog can stalk, she crept two houses down and peered around a bush.

Parker joined her. "What are we looking at?" All he saw was a scruffy lawn, an abandoned blue tricycle, and a fat yellowish cat asleep on the steps.

"Good times." Ruby sank into a crouch. "Follow my lead."

In a sudden burst, she exploded, heading straight for

the feline. Parker loped alongside. He had to admit, this strong doggie body made running fun.

At Ruby's savage growl, the cat opened its eyes so wide that Parker barked out a laugh. Seeing 160 pounds of determined dog bearing down on it, the tabby sprang directly up in the air with all four legs out.

"Woo-hoo! Cat!" cried Ruby.

"Yeah!" shouted Parker.

The thrill of the chase had caught him in its grasp. His tongue flapped from the side of his mouth like a pink flag, his legs pumped, and his world narrowed to one target.

*Cat.*

They galloped after the startled feline—up onto the stoop, through the bushes, and around and around the lawn. The dogs had longer legs, but the tabby was highly motivated. Parker's pulse pounded. A doggie smile stretched his mouth wide. He could get used to this kind of excitement.

At last, they cornered the cat by a massive oak tree. Its legs bunched, and up it sprang, high onto the trunk.

Half a second behind it, Ruby slammed into the tree, planting her forepaws as high as she could reach. With a hiss like a busted teakettle, the cat scuttled up to the nearest branch. There it crouched, wide-eyed, while its fur frizzed out like a porcupine with a perm.

"Cat! Cat! Cat!" barked Ruby. It sounded like so much fun that Parker joined in.

The tabby yowled some insults in Cat, which Parker didn't understand. But he got the gist of it.

After another minute, Ruby pushed off the tree trunk. She sneezed, licked her shoulder fur until it flattened out, and ambled off. Parker followed.

"So?" said the bigger dog. "What do ya think?"

Parker smiled, surprised by how much he'd enjoyed the chase. "Okay, that was kind of fun."

She bumped his shoulder and he staggered. "That's the spirit. Come on, I've got another treat for ya."

Stopping to smell the occasional bush or leave her mark on a downed branch, Ruby led the way. Parker was amazed to discover how much he learned by sniffing those scent posts that other dogs had marked. He got a sense of who else had come that way and how recently—sort of a smell-o-vision map of the neighborhood comings and goings.

Around the corner and up the street Ruby ambled, heading for a house Parker knew.

Old Man Haggard.

A grownup so salty and mean, he made Darth Vader look like a Cub Scout. Mr. Haggard would squirt his Super Soaker at any dog or cat foolish enough to cross his lawn.

He threw pine cones at any kid he caught walking past his house, he egged trick-or-treaters, and he'd once tried to get Parker's sister, Billie, arrested for, as he said, "looking suspicious." (She'd stopped to tie her shoe on the walk home.)

"You don't want to go there," said Parker. "He's trouble."

Ruby grinned a wolfish grin. "No, he's *in* trouble."

Parker slowed his pace. The last thing he wanted was to mix it up with Old Man Haggard. "Wait, he'll catch us—or squirt us."

The older dog checked the house and driveway. Mr. Haggard's glossy cobalt BMW was missing from its parking spot, and all the window shades were drawn. The blank-faced house looked deserted. Still, she raised her snout and sniffed the air.

"He's not home," said Ruby. "Perfect."

She padded over to the immaculate flower bed that bordered the driveway. Immaculate? Try perfect. Seriously, you could check a ruler's straightness with the edge of the bed. When Parker joined her, Ruby was scanning the plants, inhaling deeply.

"Sniffing flowers?" said Parker. He sagged a little, disappointed that her idea of fun was something so ordinary. "That's your good time?"

"Not flowers. Look!" Going rigid, Ruby stared at a hole

about the size of a golf ball. As Parker watched, a twitching nose and whiskers emerged from it, then ducked back out of sight.

"Gopher," Ruby murmured in a low growl.

"Oh, now, I don't know . . ." Uneasy, Parker checked out the house windows for any sign of movement. Still nothing.

"Kid, ya haven't lived till you've dug for gophers." Ruby's gaze was glued to the hole. "Find yourself a tunnel and see."

Wandering off, Parker scouted out the flower bed. Sure enough, almost hidden beneath some huge yellowish blooms, he spotted another hole. Feeling foolish, he watched it.

And then the strangest thing happened. Another gopher poked its face out, and Parker stiffened. His doggie body was taking over. It quivered. It yearned. He felt an overwhelming urge to pounce.

So Parker pounced.

Almost by itself, his nose jammed down into the hole, snuffling for all it was worth. The rodent was there, just beyond his reach . . .

Before he knew it, Parker found his front paws tunneling at a terrific rate. He pumped dirt behind him, spraying it left and right with wild abandon.

Yes! He was going to get that gopher!

Once more, he plunged his nose into the hole and sniffed, only to find that the gopher had fled down its tunnel. The nerve! Parker's predatory instinct was up—he barely stopped to wonder what he'd do with the little rodent if he caught it.

Nose to the ground, he waded through the flower bed in pursuit. Some part of his mind dimly protested that he shouldn't be tearing up a neighbor's garden, but Parker couldn't seem to stop. It was so cool—his keen sniffer could almost track the gopher through the earth.

When Parker caught another strong whiff of the creature, he pounced again with both forepaws, breaking through the soft earth. Once more, he dug like a belligerent bulldozer, filled with a strange kind of glee.

Time seemed to stretch . . .

"Kid? Hey, kid!" Parker became aware that Ruby was trying to get his attention.

He raised his nose, dripping with dirt. The flower bed was a disaster area—crushed blossoms, deep craters, and piles of fresh earth from all their digging. But Ruby wasn't looking at the mess. Her body was tense, her gaze fixed on the street.

"What is it?" asked Parker.

A white panel van had rounded the corner and was cruising their way.

"The Bad Man," Ruby barked. "He's seen us! Run!"

She spun and, quicker than you'd expect for a big dog, galloped off down the street.

For a long beat, Parker stayed frozen, staring. Everything seemed surreal and distant, like a movie.

"Kid!" barked Ruby.

Her urgency jolted him awake. Parker's limbs tingled with a rush of adrenaline.

And he ran.

Faster and harder than he ever had before, Parker blasted down the street. He vaulted over bushes and abandoned skateboards, paws skimming the ground. Within a handful of seconds, he'd caught up to Ruby.

Risking a glance over his shoulder, Parker checked for the van and nearly jumped out of his skin. The Animal Control truck loomed right behind them! An oval face with cold gray eyes stared out the windshield.

"Look out!" barked Parker.

Jumping a low hedge, Ruby cried, "This way!" She swerved, running alongside it and making for the rear of the house.

Brakes squealed as the van jolted to a stop. The stink of burning rubber assaulted Parker's nose.

With new urgency, he galloped after the older dog. They entered a tiled patio, blasting through some lounge chairs and scattering children's toys. Parker quickly noticed that the backyard was bordered on three sides by wooden fencing, too high to jump.

Alarm made his hackles rise. "We're cornered!"

"Not . . . yet we're not." Ruby panted. "This way." The older dog's pace was flagging, but she beelined it for the back corner of the yard.

"Hey!" a man's voice boomed behind them. "Come back here!"

As they neared the fence, Parker said, "I really hope you know where you're going."

"Have . . . some . . . faith," said Ruby between pants.

They'd almost run out of yard, and a glance behind revealed the Animal Control guy brandishing two long metal poles with loops on the ends—loops designed to wrap around their throats. If he and Ruby were captured and taken to the pound, Parker might never get his own body back.

Sucking in a breath, he kept running.

Then, just when Parker thought they were truly out of luck, the bigger dog hit the dirt chest-first, slid, and squirmed under the fence. Mere steps behind Ruby, he repeated her move. As he slid, Parker noticed two things:

One, the bottom of the fence ended about six inches off the ground.

And two, someone had dug a convenient hole under that corner.

Wriggling like a sandworm on a spree and clawing desperately at the dirt, Parker squeezed his body under the fence. Just as his front half emerged on the other side, he felt the Animal Control officer's snare brush his tail.

And then, he was through.

Legs braced wide apart, Ruby stood breathing heavily, her head down and her tongue nearly reaching the ground. Parker joined her.

From the opposite side of the fence, a series of colorful curses reached them. Apparently, the man was not a happy dogcatcher.

"Can I . . . show you a . . . good time . . . or what?" asked the older dog.

Parker looked up at her, his limbs still tingling from their close escape.

"Well, the gophers were fun. But I could skip the being chased part."

Ruby grinned. "Welcome to a dog's life."

⇦BOOF

# 12

# Poor Mr. Wuffles

Right away, Boof could tell that Gabi's mom was going to be one of his favorite people. And not just because she had the wide, friendly face of a Labrador. A curvy woman with big curly hair and an even bigger laugh, Mrs. Cortez offered him a treat as soon as he slid into the back seat of her car. Being a Good Dog—er, Boy, Boof was too polite to refuse.

He couldn't tell what sort of treat it was, but it definitely had nuts and that sugary stuff his human taste buds adored. He scarfed down the snack in seconds flat.

"Wow!" Gabi laughed. "You have a healthy appetite."

"I'm always hungry," said Boof.

"My kind of boy," said the Lab-Faced Woman.

When they reached Gabi's house, her mom led them directly to a warm, cozy kitchen nook and invited them to sit at the table.

"Does your mother know you're here?" she asked Boof.

"She knows I'm having fun," he said vaguely. In truth,

he couldn't remember what Parker's mom told him that morning about after-school plans, but he figured she'd want him to be happy. And this situation promised plenty of happiness.

Before long, Gabi's mom had set two bowls of ice cream in front of them and excused herself from the room. Gabi smiled. Boof grinned back.

"Let's eat!" he said.

He started to dip his face down into the bowl, then remembered what Gloomy Boy had told him about humans using their hands to eat. So he grabbed the bowl with both hands and brought it up to his mouth.

Velvety sweetness overflowed his tongue.

"I love this stuff!"

His family had never let him try this particular treat before, and Boof was amazed at its cool creaminess. *Yum. Humans got the best food.* He lapped up the ice cream with gusto, his mouth flooding with taste sensations. Halfway through, Boof happened to glance over at Gabi.

Her jaw hung open and a gob of ice cream rested on her spoon, forgotten. She was staring at Boof.

"What?" he asked.

"It's just—" Gabi hid a smile with her other hand. "I've never seen anyone eat ice cream that way."

He smiled back. "I'm one of a kind."

Setting down her spoon, Gabi raised a napkin in one hand. "May I?"

Boof shrugged. He had no idea what she meant.

Then the girl reached the napkin across the table and gently wiped off his nose, chin, and cheeks. "Most people use a spoon."

"I'm not most people." *Understatement of the year.*

After they finished their treat, Gabi led Boof into a comfortable room, sat down on the sofa, and turned on the picture box. When he'd been in dog form, Boof had never liked watching it, because the flickering images bugged his eyes. But seen through these human eyes, the box was a marvel. Tiny humans ran about inside it, doing strange and miraculous things.

"Want to play?" asked Gabi. She handed him a hard black object with buttons, which looked a little like the boomerang his Sweet Girl used to throw for him before she went away. Boof loved Fetch. A sharp twinge of the heart ambushed him at the thought of the Boy's littermate. He missed Sweet Girl's easy affection and her smell; he missed seeing her.

Maybe this girl could help take her place? The black thing she'd handed him was a little heavy to catch in his mouth, but perhaps he could use these human hands.

"You want to throw first?" he asked.

"Throw?" A slight crease appeared between her eyebrows, then after a long moment, Gabi laughed and pushed his shoulder. "You joker! You really had me going."

Boof chuckled in response. Maybe *he* would throw it first? He didn't know her game.

"I haven't played with this before," he said.

"Don't worry," said Gabi. "It's easy. Just hold the controller like this."

She picked up another black boomerang thingy and showed him how to make a figure move around in the picture box, jumping and running and picking things up. The point of the game, she told him, was to use your guy to collect as much treasure as possible, without being ripped off by the other treasure hunters or caught by the bad guys.

She might as well have been speaking Weasel.

Once he realized there would be no playing of Fetch, Boof's interest dimmed. It felt weird to sit still, pushing buttons to make somebody in the picture box move, instead of moving yourself. Still, he was just getting the hang of it when a faint, familiar scent teased his nose. He sniffed deeply.

It wasn't a bird, it wasn't a dog . . .

From the corner of his eye, Boof caught a flicker of movement. He turned toward the doorway.

*Cat!*

Dropping the black thingy like it was a thorny stick, Boof went rigid. "Cat!"

Gabi barely spared the creature a glance. "Oh, yeah. Don't mind Mr. Wuffles."

But Mr. Wuffles was all Boof could think about. Slowly, stealthily, he stood up. The stripy brown creature wasn't alarmed. It sauntered toward the couch, tail curling.

"Parker, your guy's getting in trouble," said Gabi, still staring at the picture box and working her boomerang.

"Uh-huh."

Crouching down, Boof gathered his strength. All his attention was focused on the cat. And then . . . he sprang!

*Whump!*

Landing off-balance, Boof accidentally caught a lamp with his elbow. Before it even hit the floor, the cat had reacted.

With a yowl, Mr. Wuffles dodged. Like a streak of brown lightning, he tore around behind the couch, with Boof hard on his tail.

"Hold still!" cried Boof.

As the cat ducked under the other end table, Boof made a grab. Mr. Wuffles escaped, but Boof's shoulder slammed into the table, toppling the other lamp. It shattered on the wood floor.

"Hey!" cried Gabi, half rising.

"Cat!" shouted Boof, in explanation.

Racing around the low table, Mr. Wuffles scampered for the doorway he'd entered through. Boof couldn't let the creature escape. He ran right over the tabletop, scattering magazines and books in his wake.

Gabi squeaked in surprise.

"What's going on in there?" came her mom's voice from deeper in the house.

"Parker, stop messing around," said Gabi.

"Why?"

"You're scaring the cat."

"That's the whole idea!" He tore out of the room and down a short hallway in pursuit.

Mr. Wuffles glanced back, eyes as big as tennis balls.

"I've got you now, cat!" cried Boof. In three long strides, he closed the distance.

But the wily feline poured on another burst of speed and vanished through a convenient doorway. Boof followed, entering a room dominated by a long table with chairs all around it. Sitting in one of them with papers spread before her was Mrs. Cortez.

Mr. Wuffles ducked under the table. Right behind him, Boof skidded onto his knees. Shoving aside a chair and hoisting the tablecloth, he saw that the cat had leaped into Mrs. Cortez's lap.

"Aha! You caught it," he said to the Lab-Faced Woman. Scrambling to his feet, Boof rounded the table.

Gabi's mother stood up, cat cradled in her arms and dark eyes flashing. "What in the world is going on here?" As Boof approached, she shifted to protect her pet.

"I was chasing the cat," he said, dancing on the balls of his feet. Boof reached out a hand, and Mr. Wuffles took a swipe at it with his paw.

"We do *not* chase cats around here," said the woman.

"Oh. Too bad."

Boof had always thought it tragically misguided that some humans would welcome a sneaky cat into their home rather than a noble dog. He snatched at the creature again, and this time, Gabi's mom spun away to protect the little rotter.

"Mr. Wuffles is like family," she said, "and you've scared him out of his wits."

"What's wrong with that?" asked Boof. Half the fun of chasing a cat was scaring it.

She straightened, shooting him a glare that outdid the cat's. "We do not scare our pets. And if you don't know how to behave properly, perhaps I should take you home now."

"No!" said Gabi, joining them.

Boof wilted under her mom's gaze. He hated it when people didn't like him.

"Your guest has been terrorizing poor Mr. Wuffles," said her mother.

The girl came to stand beside Boof. "I'm sure he didn't mean it. Parker just likes to joke around, don't you?"

It took a moment for Boof to realize that she was talking about him. "No, I really meant to chase the cat," he said.

Hurt and puzzlement were written across Gabi's face. "But why?"

Boof shrugged. "Because it's fun."

"That's it," said Mrs. Cortez. "I've heard enough. Gabi, take Mr. Wuffles to his bed. Young man, you and I are going to tell your mother and father what you've been up to."

From her tone, Boof guessed that he had been a Bad Dog. He tucked his tail (or what would've been his tail), but he really didn't see what all the fuss was about. Cats had been put into this world to give dogs something to chase, simple as that. He knew it. Everybody knew it. Even cats.

But the woman didn't seem to agree. She collected her purse and jacket, and then stood with arms crossed, watching him. Reluctantly, Gabi carried Mr. Wuffles from the room, glancing back at Boof all the while.

"Bye, I guess," she said.

"See you soon," he said, because that was the kind of thing he'd heard humans say.

"Not if I can help it," muttered Gabi's mom. "Now, Parker, what's your mom's or dad's phone number?"

Boof blinked. "Phone number?"

She made a *tsk* sound with her mouth and stuck out a hand. "Give me your phone."

Searching around himself, Boof wasn't exactly sure what she meant. Then he recalled that book bag Gloomy Boy had told him to carry around.

"Maybe it's in . . . the bag?" he guessed.

"And where's your bag?" asked Mrs. Cortez.

Boof screwed up his face and thought hard. Had he brought it with him in the woman's car? "School, maybe?"

"Does Gabi have your number?"

All Boof could offer was an elegant shrug.

Gabi's mom blew out a sigh. "All right, then, I'll take you home. What's your address?"

"Address?"

A muscle in Mrs. Cortez's jaw twitched. Her face looked a little like the Boy's had when Boof sampled those spicy noodles two nights ago. "Do you know where you live?" Her voice was tighter than a brand-new choke collar.

Boof chewed his lower lip. "I know what it looks like." When the woman squeezed her eyes shut, he added, "It's near a park. With dogs."

"Then let's go find it," said Gabi's mom.

As they climbed into the car, Boof wondered if she would give him a treat for correctly identifying his house. It seemed like something a Good Boy should get. How was he to know it would take, as Mrs. Cortez later said, "the whole frickin' afternoon"?

# PARKER ⇨

# 13

# Scent of a Mad Ferret

Listening to Boof's account of the day's activities was like riding a roller coaster blindfolded. You never knew what was coming. First up—"You bit Deke and he whimpered like a baby?"—then down—"You went back to the principal's office again?" But the news about Gabi really threw Parker for a loop.

"Wait, you actually *talked* to her?" he said as he and Boof shared snack time in the kitchen.

"Yesh," said Boof through a mouthful of leftover chicken.

"And you went on a *date* at her house?"

"Uh-huh."

Parker shook his head. "Wow. I've been trying to work up the nerve for years, and you get through on the first try?" A rush of gratitude welled up in his chest. For once, Boof was actually making his life better—if only Parker could reclaim his body to enjoy the results.

"She's nice," mumbled Boof as he crunched on a carrot. "But I think her mom hates me."

Parker slurped up some Oatios from his bowl. "Why's that?"

"I dunno. Maybe she didn't appreciate my chasing her cat?"

*Pffagh!* Parker sprayed his cereal in surprise. *"What?"*

Taking another enormous bite, Boof mumbled, "And now she doesn't—*mmf*—want me hanging out with Gabi."

Parker growled. His head felt as hot and throbbing as an infected boil. "Stay out of my love life!" he barked.

Boof's eyebrows lifted and he held up a palm. When he'd finished swallowing, he said, "But Cody said you hadn't talked to her in years."

"That doesn't matter." Parker felt like biting someone. (Someone being Boof.) But instead of doing damage to his own human body that he might later regret, he stalked off into the family room. "Stay out of it!" he called over his shoulder.

A few minutes later, Parker heard the sounds of things being returned to the fridge. At least the rotten dog had learned that much. He curled into a tight ball on the rug, griping to himself.

Before long, footsteps slapped down the hallway. When

Parker glanced up. Boof was shifting from foot to foot in the doorway, wearing a worried look.

"Are you feeling better?" asked Boof.

"No." Parker glared at the dog in human form.

"Oh. I wish you felt better."

Parker watched him, waiting for an apology. "Well?" he said at last.

Boof blinked. "Well what?"

"Aren't you going to say you're sorry?"

Boof's eyebrows drew together. "Why?"

"Because you're wrecking my life!" Parker growled. He bit back an even meaner comment and tried to cool down. A thought occurred. "Do you even know what *sorry* means?"

Boof shrugged, shaking his head.

*Oh, boy.*

As simply as possible, Parker explained that when you've done something that hurts someone else, you're supposed to apologize and try to make good. Watching Boof's face, he wasn't sure how much of it was getting through.

Parker tried another tack.

"Okay, remember when you ate my sister's cake and we were all mad at you?"

Boof had the good grace to hang his head. "Yes."

"That hurt Billie." *And me,* he thought. "And that's an

example of when you should say you're sorry. Get it?"

"Ohhh." The light of understanding dawned in Boof's eyes.

"So?" Parker sent him an expectant look.

"Oh. I'm . . . sorry?"

Parker gusted out a sigh. "Close enough." Getting to his feet, he said, "And now you can make good on your mistakes."

"How? I'll do anything to make you happy again."

"Take me to the Mystic Crystal to see if they'll help us."

Boof's face brightened. "I can do that."

After painstakingly looking up the address on the desktop computer—Boof's typing skills hadn't improved any—the pair set out. Since they'd be visiting a busier part of town, Parker made Boof attach the leash to his collar. It wouldn't do to get busted, not now.

During the long walk, a cornucopia of smells teased Parker's nose. He detected the neighbor dog Ruby behind her fence, the cat at the corner, the bitter tang of car exhaust, and the many, many people and dogs who'd walked down that sidewalk before them. But none of those smells claimed Parker's attention as thoroughly as thoughts of their destination and what might happen there.

Boof, on the other hand, was Boof. He kept trying to

sniff the bushes and complaining about his weak human nose. And every time they startled a squirrel, he'd cry, "Squirrel!" and chase it to whichever tree it had scaled. Over and over, Parker dragged him away.

After what felt like a day, but was probably only a half hour, Parker and Boof finally reached their goal.

The Mystic Crystal occupied an old-fashioned lavender-colored cottage on a corner of a popular shopping street. Its display window bristled with laughing Buddhas, sparkling geodes, dragon sculptures, and so much cool junk that Parker couldn't take it all in. This had been one of Mimi's favorite stores, and although she'd only brought him here twice before, Parker loved its aura of possibilities. The Mystic Crystal made you believe that magic was real.

Of course, having your soul transplanted into a dog's body had the same effect.

Two long wind chimes tinkled on either side of the sapphire-blue door. The woody smell of incense drifted out on a breeze, making Parker sneeze.

Boof looked at him, he looked at Boof. Together they took a deep breath and walked through the door. Aside from the incense, the shop smelled of wood, rocks, sage, and things Parker couldn't identify. Floaty flute music noodled quietly in the background, while three adults pawed through the jumbled selection of charms, necklaces, statues, and T-shirts.

"I don't see any food," said Boof, surveying the store.

"Forget your stomach for a second and focus."

"How?"

Parker considered. "Just . . . look around at all the stuff for a minute, while I try to figure out who works here."

Nodding in agreement, Boof drifted toward a tabletop display and bent to sniff a purple lampshade dripping with fringe. He sneezed and rubbed his nose. "Tickles."

Meanwhile, Parker padded over to check out the grownups—two women and one man. The man kept pulling T-shirts off the rack, holding them up to his chest, and frowning into a mirror. Parker figured him for a customer.

"—Think we've got a love charm here somewhere," one of the women was saying. She untangled a bracelet from a rack and raised it for a closer look. "Ah, here you go! The same design that Cleopatra used to charm Marc Antony."

*Bingo. This must be the store clerk.*

Parker kept an eye on her while pretending to sniff the statues. Even as he did this, he realized that fake shopping wasn't as convincing a cover when you were a dog. Sure enough, the clerk sent Parker a long, dubious look as she rang up her customer.

"Kid," she called to Boof. "Dude!" When he didn't respond, she tried the old standby, "Hey, you!"

"Boof!" said Parker. "Answer her."

Boof glanced up from a wooden statue he'd been eyeing like a new chew toy. "Hmm?"

"Keep your dog on a leash," said the worker. "He breaks it, you bought it."

That didn't sound very New Agey to Parker. But little did she know that the "boy" was more likely to mess with her merchandise than the "dog."

"Oh, okay," Boof mumbled. He strolled over, lifted the end of the leash, and stuffed it into a jeans pocket. "Check out this wood," he told Parker, holding out the statue. "That's some good chewing there."

Parker nodded, thinking, *It probably has a nice crunch.* And then he caught himself. "Don't even think of it."

Setting down the carving on a shelf, Boof said, "Relax. I'm not a total dum-dum." Parker wasn't so sure.

From their position halfway down one of the store's aisles, he watched as the woman customer left and the clerk went to help the man. After examining nearly every T-shirt in the shop, he finally dropped the last one onto his pile of discards.

"None of this is suitable," he snapped.

"Looking for a particular color, sir?" asked the clerk. "Something to enhance your aura?"

He scowled at her. "I want a sixties costume."

"A sixties costume?"

"Where's all your tie-dye? You call this a New Age store? You people should be ashamed of yourselves." And with that, he turned and flounced out the door.

Parker's sharp ears caught the store clerk's muttered complaint as the man left. Grousing to herself, she squatted in the aisle to begin the task of refolding and restoring the T-shirts to their proper places. Parker sniffed the air, scanning the store. He and Boof were the only customers left. Perfect.

"Here we go," he told Boof. "You're on."

"On what?" But Boof followed Parker up the aisle.

The clerk, a short, olive-skinned woman with a streak of purple in her dark hair, barely gave them a glance. "Help you?" she asked, continuing to fold T-shirts.

Parker told Boof what to say.

"Yes, we—um, *I* need some advice," said Boof.

Without looking, the purple-haired woman pointed to a bookcase. "Astrology books are over there. Second shelf."

"Real advice," said Parker. Boof repeated his words.

With a sigh, the clerk sat back on her heels and turned to study the pair. They must not have impressed her, because she said, "Make it snappy, little dude. I'm working."

Following Parker's instructions, Boof said, "What do you know about souls changing bodies?"

She frowned. "Excuse me?"

Boof explained that he was looking for advice on how to reverse a—"What do you call it?" he asked Parker.

"Soul swap."

Purple Hair looked from Boof to Parker and back. "You're asking your dog what to say?"

"Well, yeah," said Boof. "He knows best."

Pushing up to standing, the clerk said, "Okay, very funny. Ha-ha."

"Ha-ha?" Boof cocked his head.

"I know when I'm being pranked," said Purple Hair. "If you're not going to buy anything, just move along."

Parker growled softly. Finally they'd found someone who might be able to help, and she didn't believe them. He told the boy who was really a dog what to say next.

"I swear I'm not pranking you," Boof repeated. "We want to know how to reverse a soul swap."

Purple Hair's smirk made her opinion clear. "Sure you do," she said. "'Cause you and your dog have switched souls."

"How did you know?" Boof gaped.

"I'm psychic," she said, deadpan.

"Really?" said Boof. "What's that?"

"Go." With a shooing gesture, the clerk said, "Take your dog and go home. Stop wasting my time."

Boof turned to Parker. "She doesn't believe us."

Parker sagged. *What to say? What to do?* There must be some way to convince the woman, but Parker was drawing a complete blank.

"Maybe if we told her something that only a dog would know," said Boof.

"Something a boy couldn't guess?" Parker asked. "That's a great idea!"

Boof grinned, and Parker could've sworn his butt wiggled as if he were wagging a nonexistent tail.

"So what do we tell her?" asked Parker.

"The nose knows," said Boof. "Give her a sniff."

Narrowing her eyes, the clerk pointed at the door.

Instead of leaving, Parker stepped up and gave Purple Hair's pants and shoes a thorough sniffing, despite her resistance. As the scents and their meaning came clear to him, he described them to Boof.

"You had Mexican food for lunch," said Boof. "Fish tacos."

The clerk's confident sneer slipped a little. "Ye-e-ess," she said slowly, "but you could've been at the restaurant."

"You also have a ferret at home," said Parker. "It's old.

And it pees on your shoes when it's mad at you." Boof relayed all this.

"Shut up!" Purple Hair's jaw dropped. "How did you . . . ?"

"Soul swap," Boof explained. "He smells it and tells me. I could do it myself, but this human sniffer doesn't work so good. Got any food?"

Openmouthed, Purple Hair stared from one of them to the other.

"Is that a 'no'?" asked Boof.

Still speechless, she reached into her midnight blue apron, fished out an energy bar, and handed it over.

Parker laughed and wagged; he couldn't help it. Boof had certainly earned his treat. Yay, teamwork!

"High five!" Parker said. When Boof looked confused, Parker added, "Hold out your palm."

Doggie paw smacked against human hand. They traded grins.

"Now ask her if she knows any spells, or has any books about people switching souls," said Parker.

Through a mouthful of energy bar, Boof conveyed his request.

With an effort, the clerk got ahold of herself. "I'm not saying I believe in this . . . soul swap—only in the possibility of it."

"Okay," said Boof.

"But I have to ask." She squinted at him. "Are you a walk-in?"

"I walk every day," said Boof. "We even walked here."

Parker shook his head. "She means, did your spirit come from somewhere out there and take over my body?" He'd seen an article on walk-ins during their computer search the day before—plus, that was one of Mimi's favorite metaphysical speculations.

"Oh." Boof stuffed the last of the snack into his mouth. "No, we traded. My soul's in his body and his soul's in mine," he said, pointing at Parker.

Purple Hair's hand went to her mouth and her eyes widened. "A real soul swap."

"That's right," said Boof.

"And all that barking? He's really talking to you?" She pointed at Parker.

"Uh-huh."

Parker nodded.

An incredulous smile crept across her face. "Holy spaceballs."

"By the way, I make a much better human than he does a dog," said Boof.

"Hey!" barked Parker.

"What? It's true."

"Stay focused. Ask if she knows how to reverse this thing."

When Boof relayed his question, Purple Hair bit her lip and sucked in some air. "Sorry, little dude. We don't have any books on soul swapping, and I'm not really a witch—although I did go to community college."

Parker slumped. Of course. It was too much to hope for, that this random woman could somehow wave a wand and solve their problem. He'd been a fool to expect answers here.

"But I have read about your situation," the clerk continued.

"Oh, yeah?" said Boof.

Staring at a corner of the ceiling, the woman toyed with a strand of her hair. "From what I remember, this kind of thing usually happens because of a curse or a wish. Is there some magical person who's all ticked off at you?"

Parker and Boof both shook their heads.

"Then unless you angered some mystical being without knowing it, one of you probably made a wish."

Boof and Parker exchanged a glance. "Not me," said Boof.

Parker dropped his gaze to the floor. He was remembering when he and Boof were tussling over Mimi's gift.

Could that Eshu statue be inhabited by some kind of spirit? One that didn't like its home being played with?

Or . . . wait a second.

A queasy sensation rose from Parker's gut, like that time he'd eaten an entire pack of Double Stuf Oreos in a day. Hadn't he wished that Boof would have to handle an undisciplined dog so he would know how Parker felt?

"What is it?" asked Boof.

Parker wrinkled his nose. "I . . . may have made a sort-of wish."

"What sort of a sort-of wish?" asked Boof.

Following their back-and-forth, Purple Hair leaned forward in fascination. "Did your dog make the wish?"

"He's not my dog," said Boof, "he's my Boy."

"Oh, no." Parker's tail drooped. "Maybe this is all my fault."

Stooping to pet his back, Boof said, "It'll be okay. You'll see."

"How will it be okay?" Parker asked.

"I dunno, it just will."

Try as he might, Parker couldn't see it. A little groan escaped his lips.

"Don't be sad," said Boof. "I've had fun being a human."

Parker just shook his head. All the frustration, all the heartache, all the messiness—all this was his own fault?

Turning to the clerk, Boof said, "Hey, if he made a wish and we traded souls, couldn't he make another wish and put us back the way we were?"

Purple Hair scratched her chin. "Well, theoretically . . ."

"Yes?" said Parker, forgetting she couldn't understand him.

"There's a chance it might work."

That was all he needed to hear. "Let's go, Boof!" he cried, trotting to the door with the leash dragging behind him.

"Where are we going?" Boof trailed in his wake.

"Back to how we used to be."

PARKER ⇨

# 14

# Gone Wishin'

"Hey," said Boof as they hurried along the street. "We did good in there."

"We sure did," said Parker. "Teamwork!"

"You and me together." Boof's eyes sparkled. "And *I* did good, didn't I?"

"Totally," said Parker. "You were a really big help. Good dog." When he noticed the hopeful expression on Boof's face, he added, "But you already got your treat."

Boof shrugged, as if it was always worth a try.

Heading home, their pace seemed faster. For the first time since their transformation, Parker felt real hope blooming inside him. The brief feeling he'd experienced after reading that goofy incantation off the internet was nothing compared to this.

*This* could really work.

Loping ahead and returning, Parker kept urging Boof onward whenever the dog in human form got distracted.

And he was distracted a lot.

So wouldn't you know it, trouble came when Parker had pulled about a half block ahead. The smell arrived first—a familiar oil-and-machine scent drifting past his nose. Then brakes squealed as a vehicle pulled to the curb.

Swinging around, Parker felt his legs go weak at the sight of it.

The Animal Control van.

And it was between him and Boof.

A thick man in a tan uniform hopped from the van onto the sidewalk. He was normal height but double wide, as if someone had started pumping helium into his body and forgot to stop. His jowly, oval face wore a dark scowl as if it were the latest style. One hand held a doggie treat, the other held a snare.

"Come here, poochie," called the man in a surprisingly high voice.

"Boof! Hey, Boof!" barked Parker. But his friend was absorbed in watching a squirrel climb an oak.

Parker hesitated, torn. Should he try to rejoin Boof or run home?

The dogcatcher eased closer, his lips crimped up at the corners in a poor imitation of a smile. "Come here, you mutt," he murmured, extending the hand with the treat in it. "This time, you're mine."

Parker tried to circle the man and return to Boof, but Mr. Double-Wide hopped across the sidewalk, arms spread, and Parker had to retreat into someone's front yard.

When Parker tried again to get past him, the man feinted to the right with the snare, but slid to the left, stepping closer. Parker scrambled back into some low bushes. For a big guy, Mr. Double-Wide was light on his feet.

Attempting another dodge, Parker circled back the other way and was jerked to a rude halt. He glanced behind him. His leash had snagged on a branch.

"Now I gotcha." The dogcatcher grinned a grin empty of any humor. He marched forward, gray eyes as hard as granite pebbles.

"Boof!" Parker barked his loudest. "Help!"

At last, Boof heard. Reading the situation at a glance, he hustled over to join them.

"Stay back, boy." The man scowled at him. "This stray might could have rabies. Or mange."

"This dog?" said Boof. "He's no stray. He's the best dog in the world."

Despite himself, Parker felt a warm glow at Boof's words. He still thought Boof was laying it on a bit thick, but given the situation, he took the compliment.

"This your dog?" asked Mr. Double-Wide.

"Yup." Strolling up to Parker, Boof unsnarled the leash and petted him on the head. "Who's a good little Parkie Warkie?" he cooed, in a fair imitation of Billie's voice.

"Shouldn't ought to let him off leash," said the dogcatcher. Parker could practically smell disappointment and frustration rising from him in a funk.

"He's not off leash," said Boof, holding up the lead. "He was wearing it all the time."

Mr. Double-Wide's mouth narrowed to a thin line. After two days of talking with Boof, Parker knew how the guy felt.

"You know what I mean," said the dogcatcher, his voice tighter than Jabba the Hutt's jockstrap. "You gotta control the dog at all times. That's the law."

"Parker's a Good Dog," said Boof. "He'd never break the law."

"Oh, yeah?" The man sneered. "I seen him running around the streets earlier today with some other mutt."

"Really?" Boof asked Parker.

"I—yeah. Tell you later," Parker replied, jerking his head toward Mr. Double-Wide. "He doesn't know we can talk, remember?"

"Oh, right," said Boof. He slipped his hand through the loop in the leash. "Well, gotta go," he told the man. "Those treats won't eat themselves."

As Parker and Boof headed down the sidewalk, the dogcatcher called after them, "I got my eye on that dog. If I catch him again, he's going straight to the pound."

Parker cast a worried glance behind. Boof, however, just kept walking, raising his hand and wiggling his fingers *toodle-oo.*

⇧⇩

The encounter with the dogcatcher lit a fire under Parker. He tugged Boof the rest of the way home, eager to find Mimi's statue and wish himself back into his normal body. Being a dog had serious consequences.

Back home, Parker persuaded Boof to postpone dinnertime and instead detoured into the dining room. They gazed up at the hutch. The statue wasn't sitting in its usual place.

Parker gasped.

"Where is it?" asked Boof.

For a moment, blind panic twisted Parker's stomach into a sailor's knot. And then he remembered: He had slept with the carving after he and Boof squabbled over it the other night. It had fallen to the floor . . .

"Let's go," he said.

Leading the way, Parker charged up the stairs and into his bedroom. He inhaled deeply, catching a whiff of that rich woody smell from somewhere in the mess that Boof had made of his room. With his powerful sniffer, it was short work to locate the carving under a dirty T-shirt beside the bed.

Parker carefully took the statue into his mouth. He didn't want to scar it any worse than Boof already had.

"How do we do this?" asked Boof.

"I *mm*-fink I just *mm*-wishf," Parker said around the hunk of wood between his teeth.

"Should I touch it too?"

After weighing this idea for a moment, Parker said, "*Mm*-okay."

Boof gripped the end that protruded from Parker's mouth. "Ready."

Closing his eyes, Parker took a deep breath. This was it. All he had to do was make a wish and everything would return to normal. He tried to clear his mind of distracting thoughts.

But a smell kept intruding like a curious cat begging for attention. A familiar sandalwood scent, from the statue itself.

Mimi's smell.

In a blink, his throat squeezed tight and his eyes prick-led. Parker didn't know if dogs could cry, but he just might be the first. Plus, he felt compelled to put that dirty T-shirt into the laundry hamper. Shaking off the distraction, Parker sucked in another breath.

"Are we done?" asked Boof.

Parker shook his head no. Once more, he tried to center himself. He thought, *I wish I was back in my own body again, and that Boof was back in his.*

For a long moment, he froze, waiting for . . . something. A sign? But nothing happened.

Parker opened his eyes. He was still in a dog's body, still biting a statue that had been who knew where.

"Nothing, huh?" said Boof, releasing his grip.

Gently, Parker set down the carving. "Nothing."

Rubbing his hands together, Boof said, "Okay. You know where to find me." And out the door and down the stairs he went.

Parker sagged. A part of his mind said, *Maybe it'll happen overnight, like last time.* But a bigger part knew that the transformation couldn't possibly be that easy, that he was trapped in doggie form until . . . until something happened.

He wished Mimi were here. She'd know what to do.

As the inevitable wave of sadness swamped him, he gave a low moan. It was enough to drive a dog—or a human stuck in a dog's body—to despair. With a mournful sigh, Parker surveyed the room, lifted the discarded T-shirt in his teeth, and began tidying up Boof's mess.

⇧⇩

An hour or two later—it was hard to judge time while in dog mode—Parker's parents came home, bringing with them the smells of moo shu pork, Szechuan chicken, and other yummy Chinese dishes. His stomach gurgled like a storm drain after a rain.

Ensconced in the family room, Parker had pulled down all the fantasy books he could reach. He was pawing through them, searching for clues on how to reverse his transformation, when his mom passed by the doorway.

"Is that dog . . . reading?" She paused and stared, arms laden.

Boof popped up beside her. "Him? Uh . . ."

Parker knew he was a terrible liar. "Tell her you were working on a school project," he said, licking a forepaw to look more doglike.

"Yeah, that's my school project," said Boof. "I was, um, reading him stories. He liked them."

"Nice save," said Parker.

"Oh-kayyy . . ." said his mom. "Don't forget to put those books back."

"So, what's new?" Boof asked Parker's mom. He was beginning to pick up more human greetings and common sayings.

"Did you forget?" She kissed Boof on the cheek, and

Parker felt a twinge of—not exactly jealousy, but a kind of yearning. The dog wearing his body was getting all the affection that should've been Parker's, while the real Parker was still invisible to his parents.

And nothing he'd found in his books would help change that.

"Forget what?" Boof followed her into the kitchen.

A whiff of anger reached Parker's sensitive nose as he trailed behind them.

His mother stood with her hands on her hips, staring at the chaos Boof had created on the table and counter. "Parker, honestly! Our friends are coming over for dinner in an hour, and this is how you help us prepare?"

Parker winced. He'd been so occupied with the bedroom and his research, he'd forgotten to check for other messes. Boof slouched there, wearing his *so what's that got to do with me* expression, watching Parker's mother for a clue.

"Say you're sorry," said Parker.

"Huh?" Boof glanced down, then caught his meaning. "Oh. Uh, I'm sorry, Mom."

Affection and irritation warred on Parker's mother's face. She shook her head. "I don't know what's gotten into you lately. You're like a different person."

Boof shrugged.

"Help me clean this up," she said.

Clumsily, Boof lent a hand, although Mom had to dictate his every action. Parker could tell that the very concept of cleaning up was as strange to him as disco dancing was to a duck. But to be fair, Boof made an effort.

After the kitchen had been restored to order, Parker's mom shooed them out into the family room to reshelve the books. Parker was relieved to hear that Boof wouldn't be attending his parents' dinner party. That was the surest recipe for disaster he could think of.

They had just shelved the last book, when the desktop computer played a little musical riff. Boof glanced around, puzzled.

"It's Skype," said Parker. "Someone's calling us." He hopped off the sofa and trotted over to the computer, gazing up at the screen. "It's Billie. Answer it!"

Boof stepped over to the desk. At Parker's direction, he clicked the mouse on the button that opened the connection. Up popped Billie's image.

"P-man!" she cried, her face lighting up.

"My Sweet Girl!" said Boof. If he'd had a tail, it would have been wagging. "Where are you?"

"'Girl'?" she teased. "I'm four years older than you. And you know where I am, you nut."

"Ask her, how's Ireland?" said Parker, rearing up and planting his forepaws on the desktop.

"Boofie-woofie!" Billie's smile split her face. "Oh, I miss you guys so much."

"I miss you too," barked Parker. She laughed to hear it, and his heart gave a leap like a dancing dolphin.

"How's, um, Eye-land?" asked Boof. He looked like he was about to lick her face on the computer screen, so Parker put a restraining paw on his arm.

"Only totally amazing," said Billie. "They've got auditions for a musical tomorrow, and I'm going to try out for it. *Squee!*"

As she burbled on about her experiences in Ireland, Parker and Boof edged closer to the screen, shoulder to shoulder. A lump formed in Parker's throat, and he wished he could tell Billie all that had happened to him since she left.

Guilt knifed through his gut. He'd been so absorbed in his own problems, Parker hadn't even thought of her and whatever challenges she was facing.

"Come home," said Boof. "Now."

Billie laughed again. "You know I won't be home till Christmas."

"Is that a long time?" asked Boof.

"Uh, yeah." She gave him a funny look.

"Longer than two sleeps?"

Nudging the doggish boy with his shoulder, Parker said, "Don't talk like that. She'll think I'm mental."

Billie frowned. "Everything okay, bro? Is middle school all right?"

Boof half grimaced. "Kind of. It's hard, and I don't understand much. But they seem to like me."

"That's good."

"Except for the teacher."

"I see," said Billie.

"And the principal. Oh, and the mom of the girl whose cat I chased."

At the reminder of Boof's disastrous visit with Gabi, Parker let his chin drop to the desktop with a *thunk*. After all their recent camaraderie, he'd almost forgotten that Boof was busy turning him into a social outcast. Accidentally, but still.

Billie chuckled. "Looks like even Boof is embarrassed for you. Don't worry. I'm sure it's not as bad as you think."

"Okay," said Boof, but he didn't sound sure.

Parker wondered if he'd ever be able to repair the damage Boof was causing to his reputation and grade point average. He wondered if he'd ever get back into his own body.

The wish he'd made on the statue just had to work.

It *had* to.

Without his intending it, a low doggie moan escaped his lips.

"Aw, Boofie," said Billie. "My sweet puppy. I miss you like mad." She leaned closer to the camera lens and made smoochie sounds.

"I miss you too," said Boof, licking the screen. He turned to Parker. "Don't you miss her?"

"Every single day." Parker's chest felt dense and his vision blurred. Pushing off the desktop, he curled up in a corner of the room to nurse his heavy heart.

If the wish didn't work and his fantasy research failed him, he didn't know what he would do.

⇦BOOF

# 15

# Friends Left and Right

After a good meal, nothing hit the spot like a nice, vigorous round of Ball. Boof loved the running around; it helped his food settle properly. But when he came into the kitchen and asked Parker's father to play, the man sent him a strange look and kept filling skinny glasses with some bubbly liquid.

"Bird, didn't you notice our friends in the dining room? What exactly makes you think this is a good time to play catch?"

The man's voice had an edge to it. Didn't he love Boof? Worried, Boof decided to try out the new word Parker had taught him. "I'm, um, sorry?"

"It's okay, little man." The Boy's dad set the glasses onto some flat, platelike thing and picked it up. "Maybe we can play tomorrow."

When Boof asked the woman, she barked out a laugh. "Not the best timing, honey," she said, pulling some dishes out of the big silver warming box. It all smelled amazing, and Boof wanted to stay and sample it, but she shooed him out of the kitchen. "Why don't you go play fetch with Boof? I'm sure he could use the exercise."

Now that Boof had worked his way through the pack hierarchy, he would play with the one who needed it the most. He and Parker had had some good times today, but for some reason, the Boy had turned sulky again. Who knew why? Maybe he wasn't fully appreciating how awesome it was to be a dog?

No matter. Boof would cheer him up.

He found Parker in the backyard, standing on the grass and staring at the moon. With his drooping tail and wet, amber eyes, the Boy looked sadder than a box of orphaned puppies.

"I know just what you need," said Boof.

"A complete reboot of my life?"

"No, this."

Boof scooped the ball off the grass and bounced it right in front of the Boy's nose. That move never failed to get *him* going. He was sure it would work on Parker.

Nothing.

"Hey, Grumpy Face, let's play," said Boof.

"Not in the mood."

Waving the ball just out of reach, Boof said, "Come on, I know you want to."

Parker looked away. "You don't know anything."

Gloomy Boy was missing the point. Play always made you feel better. Didn't he understand this? "I know you like Ball," said Boof. "Every dog likes to play Ball."

"I'm *not* a dog!" Parker blew out some air. "Look, that wish I made on the statue is our last hope."

"Yeah?" Boof wasn't sure what the Boy was driving at.

"If it doesn't work, I'm fresh out of ideas. We could be stuck like this forever."

Boof waggled the ball invitingly. "All the more reason to play. If you're a dog forever, you've gotta have fun with it."

"No, thanks."

Boof cocked his head. The Boy really wasn't getting it. Squatting down, Boof tossed the ball from hand to hand right in front of Parker's nose, chanting, "Ball! Ball! Ball! Ball!"

"Enough!" Parker growled, twisting away. "You don't know me. You don't know what I need."

Stung, Boof said, "I know you need to lighten up."

"Lighten up? Lighten *up*?" Gloomy Boy paced back and forth, his words erupting hot and fast. "You're not taking my life seriously, you ding-dong. Wrecking my reputation at school? Getting a date with the girl I like and then making her hate me? You're ruining my life."

Boof found his hands clenching into fists. It hurt that Parker didn't seem to love him but his gut was hotter than the night he swallowed spicy noodles. Was this some human thing? He couldn't stop the spill of angry words. "Oh, yeah? Your life was wrecked to begin with."

"What?!"

"Ever since I got here, you've been Gloomy Boy."

"Have not!"

"Have so! You're always moping around, cleaning things."

Parker gaped. "I lost my favorite person in the world. And then you came along—'Ooh, look at me, I'm so cute!'—taking all of Billie's attention. So I lost that too."

"*I* took it?" said Boof, his voice rising. He couldn't seem to stop talking. "You're the one."

"Me?"

"She wouldn't play with me, she wouldn't walk me. And you're all 'I'm so sad, take care of me.' So she did."

Parker snorted. "No way. She talked to you more on the Skype call."

"That's 'cause you can't talk human anymore," said Boof.

"You're impossible!"

"You're ridiculous!"

They glared at each other, the ball lying forgotten between them in the dead grass.

"She always liked you best," said Parker.

"She always liked *you* best," said Boof.

"Augh!" Parker tossed his head. "I can't talk to you anymore."

Sticking out his tongue, Boof said, "You're a doo-doo head." *Where did that come from?*

"And you're just a dumb dog, no matter whose body you're wearing." Nose in the air, Parker spun and padded toward the back door.

"Where are you going?" asked Boof.

"To get some sleep," said the Boy. "And hopefully when I wake up, this will all have been a bad dream."

*Thup-thup* went the doggie door. And he was gone.

Boof's throat felt choked, and he noticed a strange prickling behind his eyes. He wanted to hit something, he wanted to run away, and he wanted to howl like a broken-hearted wolf.

What were all these strange feelings? Why hadn't playing Ball worked? Boof hadn't made Parker any happier; in fact, he'd driven him away. Boof hung his head.

It was much harder being human than he had ever imagined.

⇧⇩

When the next day dawned with Boof and Parker still in the wrong bodies, Gloomy Boy refused to speak. He didn't scold Boof about picking up his clothes or washing his hands; he didn't beg him for human food. He just did his business behind the bushes out back, ate his dog food without comment, and curled up in the corner.

After many failed attempts to engage the Boy, Boof gave up.

Fine. If Parker wanted to sulk and moan, Boof didn't need him. He had better things to do, better people to spend time with.

But underneath, it stung. After their adventures yesterday, Boof had thought he and the Boy were finally becoming friends, finally growing close.

The ends of his mouth turned down, all on their own. Living as a human in the human world was more confusing than trying to have a conversation with a crow. Most of the time he had no idea why humans did what they did.

He didn't think *they* knew either.

After breakfast, Boof took Parker for a short walk. The Boy was still giving him the silent treatment. As he got ready to go to school, Boof thought he might welcome its mysteries and challenges for a change.

Wading through the usual chaos that greeted him

when Parker's dad dropped him at the school gate, Boof gave himself a talking-to. *Cheer up,* he thought. *Being a human isn't that hard.* After all, he'd learned to walk on two legs and open the big white food box, hadn't he? If Boof was stuck in this body for good, he'd make the most of it. He'd be the best human ever.

Today he didn't see Cody waiting for him in the hall, but Boof wasn't worried. By now, he knew just where to go. He threaded his way through all the kids heading for class without even once bending to sniff anybody's crotch.

Boof gave himself a mental pat on the back. *Who's a Good Boy?* His butt wiggled.

When he rounded a corner, there stood the Rottweiler-faced boy he'd bitten yesterday. Boof slowed his steps. You never knew how someone would react to being bitten.

"Oh, hey, Parker," said Deke. Unlike yesterday, he was smiling and friendly.

Boof relaxed a little. "Hello, you."

The big boy stepped closer. "No hard feelings about yesterday, right?"

"Uh, right." Boof wasn't entirely sure what he meant.

"I stepped out of line, and you bit me," said Deke. "Water under the bridge."

Glancing around, Boof didn't notice any water, nor did he see a line. But he'd learned that humans often talked about things you couldn't see or smell. "Water and the bridge."

Deke held out his hand.

For a moment, Boof was puzzled, but then he remembered Sweet Girl trying to teach him that trick. He held out his own hand and moved it up and down with Deke's.

Strange custom.

Now that he was closer, he noticed that Deke was smiling with his mouth but not his eyes. Unsure how to read that, he wondered if Rottweiler Boy was sad about something.

"Hey, we used to be friends when we were younger," said Deke.

"We did?" said Boof. Maybe that was the reason for his sadness?

"We should be friends again."

This sounded wonderful to Boof. The more friends, the better, as far as he was concerned. If everybody loved him, he would be the happiest Dog—er, Boy around.

"Okay with me," he said.

Deke clapped him on the shoulder, a little hard, and Boof staggered a step to recover. "So why don't you come over to my place after school?" said the big boy. "We'll play some games and set things straight."

"Games?" Boof brightened. "Like Ball?"

"Sure, I love playing ball. I've got a killer arm."

If Boof still had a tail, it would've been wagging. "It's so hard to find someone to play."

Deke glanced around the crowded hallway. "Come over around three thirty or so, and we'll play hard. You remember where I live?"

"Uh . . ."

"Never mind, I'll write it down for you." Rottweiler Boy scratched a stick across a slip of paper and handed it over. "It's not so far from your house. See you then?"

"Yes," said Boof. "We'll play Ball!"

And again, there was that smile that didn't quite reach the eyes. "Catch you later," Deke said before lumbering off down the hall.

*How about that?* thought Boof. *I'm making friends left and right.*

⇧⇩

When he reached the classroom door, Boof noticed Gabi glance at him and then away. Her face seemed tight and her mouth turned down. Boof was about to go check on the bird in the cage, but he felt a wave of that Bad Dog feeling, somehow relating to Gabi. And then he remembered what the Boy had said to do when you hurt someone.

Had he hurt Gabi? Maybe this was the right time to use

his new word? He walked over to Gabi's desk and stood waiting until she looked up at him.

"I'm sorry," he said, and he realized he meant it. Maybe Boof didn't get why Gabi was upset about his chasing that cat, but he didn't want her to be upset because of him.

"Okay . . ." she said.

Was she expecting something more? "Uh, I . . . I wanted to play with your cat, but maybe the cat didn't want to play."

Gabi's expression hovered somewhere between a frown and a smile. "Normal people don't play with cats like that," she said.

"I'm not normal people," said Boof.

Now she did smile. "That's for sure. My mom was pretty salty. She loves that cat more than me."

"Um, sorry?" Boof figured that if saying the word once was good, then twice would be even better.

Gabi flapped a hand. "She'll get over it. To tell the truth, our cat is kind of a brat. I think he needed to get shaken up a little."

"So . . . is everything okay?" Boof asked.

"Just about," she said. But then she pointed a finger at him. "As long as you promise never to chase my cat again."

"Promise," he said. After all, plenty of other cats in the world needed chasing.

They talked a little more, and Gabi said they should "hang out" at the "mall" this "weekend." Boof had no idea what all that meant, but if she was happy, then he was happy. He took his seat and began his school day on a note of hope.

*Well, look at me,* he thought. *Acting like a regular human.*

## PARKER⇨

## 16

# A World-Class Funk

Parker thought he'd known what misery was. After all, he'd been bullied off and on for years. He'd had his best friend move away, his sister leave for a semester abroad, and his beloved Mimi die—all while starting middle school, the birthplace of misery.

But those were just warm-ups for the desolation he felt now, knowing he was trapped in a dog's body for the rest of his life.

All day long, Parker moped around the house, only stirring to drink water or do his business outside. Then he'd return to his corner of the kitchen, flop down, and brood.

Parker's chest felt numb. His limbs were heavier than a drowsy dragon's.

His life was over.

He would never hug his parents again, never joke with his sister. Never play video games, or read books, or enjoy a fresh peach pie. He wouldn't even get to celebrate his upcoming birthday. It would be dog food and fleas and pooping outdoors, for the rest of his life.

The only tiny ray of hope he could spy was this: He wouldn't have to suffer forever. After all, dogs had a much shorter life span than humans.

Yay, short life span.

By the time Boof came home from school, Parker had worked himself into a world-class funk. Boof, as usual, was all enthusiasm and energy.

"Hey, Gloomy Boy!" he said, bounding into the kitchen. "Another terrific day, eh?"

Lying on the floor without moving, Parker gave him some serious stink eye. It bounced right off. Boof was the definition of oblivious.

Following his new routine, Boof opened up the fridge and piled on the snacks, shooting concerned glances at Parker. He was getting better at opening jars, so this snack session included peanut butter, pickles, leftover Chinese food, and ice cream, a new favorite. Both parents were working, so no one was around to discourage Boof's unusual eating habits.

"Want some?" asked Boof, filling his mouth.

Parker didn't respond.

"Come on. It always cheers me up when Sweet Girl

shares with me." Boof dangled a morsel of moo shu pork before Parker's nose.

Despite the delectable smell, Parker turned away.

When the gluttony was nearly over, Boof fished a slip of paper from his pocket and showed it to Parker. "Where is this?" he asked. "Is it close?"

Parker said nothing.

"Is it far?"

Still Parker said nothing.

"Oh, come on," said Boof. "You've got to talk to me sometime."

Parker snorted. "Wanna bet?" Then he realized he'd just spoken. Dang. So much for the silent treatment.

With a grin, Boof said, "That's more like it. I'm glad you're happy again. So how do I get to this place?"

Reluctantly, Parker scrutinized the scrap of paper. The address seemed familiar. "It's just past the park," he said. "Take the first street on the right."

"Will do." Boof frowned. "Which way is right again?"

Blowing out a sigh, Parker nodded at Boof's right hand.

"Right, right," said Boof. He brightened. "Hey, I made a funny. Right *right*!"

Against his will, Parker asked, "And why are you going there?"

Boof stuffed the paper back into his pocket. “Deke wants to play Ball.”

*“Deke?”* Parker sat up.

“Yes, he loves Ball.” Picking up some lo mein noodles with his fingers, Boof slurped them down. “Unlike some people.”

“Deke would never in a million years invite me over to play,” said Parker. “He hates me.”

Boof shrugged. “Well, he likes me.”

“Impossible.”

“Everybody likes me,” said Boof.

Parker ground his teeth together. “If Deke invited you over, he just wants to beat you up.”

Boof scoffed. “Shows what you know. Deke said that he stepped on a line, or something.”

“Stepped on a line?”

“Water went under a bridge,” said Boof. “Anyway, he wants to be friends again, the way we—you—used to be.”

Like a hobbit wandering the mines of Moria, Parker was getting a bad feeling about this. “Oh, no. You can’t go over there.”

Standing up, Boof said, “I can.”

“You won’t.”

“I will,” said Boof. “We will play Ball forever.”

Surging to his feet, Parker growled. "Don't be stupid. He's just going to hurt you."

Boof drew himself up and leveled a haughty look at Parker. "You don't know everything. Deke is my friend now. A better friend than you."

"You're nuts."

Lifting his chin, Boof turned and marched for the front door. "You call me bad names. You won't play with me. Deke will."

"I'm telling you he won't!" When Boof kept right on walking, Parker said, "Fine. Go on over there and get beat up. See if I care!"

"I will!" snapped Boof.

The door whipped open and slammed, and he was gone.

The quiet was deafening.

After their argument, Parker pulsed with enough energy to power a medium-sized starship. He was so antsy, he didn't even try cleaning up Boof's mess. Pacing up and down the hallway, he replayed Boof's words in his head.

*You don't know everything. Deke is my friend now.*

"What a dope," he muttered. "Dumb dog doesn't see what people are really like."

Boof at Deke's house? Parker pictured the scene. The bully would be all smiles at first, saying nice things and acting friendly. Then, when Boof's guard was down, *POW!* He'd beat him up, or torture him in some cruel, creative way. Boof would be crying before the hour was up.

*Serves him right*, he thought.

But there wasn't much heat to it.

In fact, the more Parker considered the situation, the worse he felt. Boof was just an innocent dog. Obnoxious as heck? Sure. Completely undisciplined? Absolutely. But innocent. He didn't understand people's dark side. He didn't deserve being pounded with those big fists of Deke's.

Boof had been a human for barely three days, so how was he supposed to know all the subtleties it had taken Parker twelve years of painful experience to learn?

And now he was trotting over to the bully's house like a happy calf to an all-beef barbeque.

Parker growled in frustration. *I should go after him*, he thought.

But then a face came to mind, a jowly face with chilly gray eyes.

The Animal Control officer.

If Mr. Double-Wide captured Parker, that was it. Game over. He'd head straight to the pound—no passing Go, no collecting two hundred dollars. And who knew whether Parker's parents would learn where he was in time?

Parker hung his head and gave a low moan.

*What to do?*

Pacing around the house with unseeing eyes, he passed by Mimi's favorite chair in the family room, and her familiar sandalwood scent enveloped him like a hug. He was so worked up, the smell didn't even make him want to clean things.

*What would Mimi have done?* he wondered.

And then, without even thinking, he knew. Family always came first with Mimi, no matter how many exotic trips she took or how much work loaded down her plate. Family was number one, and Boof, like it or not, was family.

Parker shook his head. *That rotten dog.*

Boof was going to get himself into some real trouble at Deke's, no doubt about it. And if that was the case, Parker had no choice.

He would hope for the best and take the risk.

He was going after him.

PARKER⇨

# 17

# A Double-Wide Disaster

In a hot minute, Parker had popped through the doggie door into the backyard and squeezed under the fence into Ruby's yard. The older dog was snoozing in a patch of afternoon sunshine, but at the noise, she surged up onto her feet.

"Intruder!" she barked. "Back off, or face my chompers!"

Parker retreated a step. "Whoa, Ruby, it's me."

Her barking continued unabated. "I'll tear ya limb from limb! I'll moidlerize ya!"

"It's me, Parker. From next door?"

The barking stopped.

Ruby blinked, finally recognizing him. "Oh, hey, kid." She yawned and shook herself. "Ya know better than to interrupt my nap."

"Sorry," said Parker, "but it's an emergency."

The Great Pyrenees cocked her colossal head. "What's up?"

"Boof is in trouble. I have to go save him."

"You?" said Ruby. Her expression was skeptical. "Pardon my saying, but you're not exactly an attack dog, kiddo."

"Doesn't matter. I still have to help him." Parker slipped past her, heading for the hedge at the back of Ruby's yard.

"No offense," said Ruby, "but ya got kind of a goofy face."

"Whatever," said Parker. "I'm going." He searched for the spot in the hedge where they'd slipped out only yesterday.

"Wait up," called Ruby.

He turned around. "You going to help me?"

"Nah, it's your fight. But I can help ya get there safely."

Parker felt absurdly grateful that the huge Great Pyrenees was coming along. He knew that two dogs could encounter just as much trouble as one, but her bulky presence was a comfort. They wiggled under the hedge together, Parker in the lead.

When they emerged into the alley, Ruby checked both directions. "Okay, all clear. Which way?"

"Over here." Setting a brisk pace, Parker trotted toward the cross street where it intersected the alley. "Hurry up!"

"Hang on," said Ruby. "Better safe than sorry."

Vibrating with impatience, Parker waited for her at the intersection. He hoped he could still catch Boof, but what if the fool had run all the way to Deke's? What then?

They lay low in the alley's mouth, waited for a car to pass, and then followed it toward the street that ran in front of the Pitts' house.

"Why the rush?" asked Ruby.

"You don't know Boof," said Parker. "He's too trusting, and this time he trusted the wrong person. He could get hurt."

Parker kept picturing that big fist headed for Boof's face—heck, *his* face, come to think of it. He picked up the pace.

When they reached the main street, all looked normal. A handful of cars. Two kids riding bikes. A woman pushing a stroller down the sidewalk.

But no Boof.

Urgency gripped Parker like an unseen fist. Suddenly he could wait no longer.

"Thanks, Ruby, but I gotta go," he said, loping off down the street.

Ruby had stopped to pee on a bush. "Sure ya don't need me?"

"I'm sure."

"Watch yourself, kid," she called after him.

As he opened up his stride, Parker felt the way he imagined a stunt driver would feel, trading a sluggish sedan for a race car. His muscles flexed and stretched. His long legs ate up the distance, and his heart pumped like a champion.

One thing was for sure: No matter what he thought about being a dog, it sure felt good to *run*.

In a flash, Parker blasted past the woman with the stroller. She shrieked, reaching down and snatching her bundled baby to her chest.

"Runaway dog!" she cried. "Look out!"

Oh, great. Now she'd called attention to him.

Didn't matter, didn't change things. Parker ran on.

After another block, the road curved. Now he could see the park ahead on the left. And on the right, far up the sidewalk, a boy's figure, jogging along.

Boof.

Relief made his limbs lighter than a balsa-wood basketball. Parker slowed his pace a little to catch his breath, knowing he'd arrive in time after all.

And then a motor gunned behind him. A familiar white van blew past, screeching to a stop just ahead in a swirl of motor-oil stink. Out jumped a familiar double-wide figure in a tan uniform.

The dogcatcher.

His gray eyes gleamed like sunlight on a knife blade. The snare in his hand trembled with anticipation.

"Come to daddy," he crooned.

Parker darted into the road, trying to pass around the van. A horn blared, and a car swerved, barely missing him.

*Yikes.*

He dodged back the other way.

This time, Mr. Double-Wide was waiting. He charged forward. The snare swung down.

Just in time, Parker ducked his head. The loop passed by so closely, it nicked his ear. Off to the right he bounded, and the man's outstretched hand barely brushed his side.

This slow human would never catch him. Just as Parker gathered himself for another burst of speed, he happened to glance down the sidewalk. Now past the park, the figure of Boof was turning onto a side street.

Deke's street.

He was too late!

As Parker lunged, the snare whipped down from behind in a blur, right over his head. He bulled forward, but the woven steel cord squeezed his neck, jerking him to a stop.

"Let me go!" he choked out. Up ahead, the boy's figure disappeared around the corner. Parker barked in a frenzy. "Boof! Boof!"

But the boy didn't hear him.

A hand gripped the scruff of his neck and a high voice rasped just behind his head. "Shut your yap. You ain't going nowhere."

Parker twisted, struggling to break free, but the snare tightened until he had trouble breathing. A muscular arm wrapped around his belly, and suddenly, Parker was hoisted into the air, four legs flailing.

"The less you struggle, the more you can breathe," said Mr. Double-Wide, jerking the snare tighter.

"I'd breathe easier if your breath wasn't so stinky." Parker gasped. Too bad the man couldn't understand him.

Something beeped close at hand, and Parker heard the van's automatic door slide open. Stepping up into the storage area, the dogcatcher lugged him inside. A cage door yawned. Before Parker could react, the man had slipped the noose off his neck, slung him into the cage, and slammed the door.

*Bam!*

Parker flung himself against the bars.

"Let me out!" he barked. The bars held firm.

Just as he realized he should think like a human—focus on undoing the latch instead of using brute force—Parker heard the lock snick shut.

Squatting down, the Animal Control worker eyed his captive. "I told your owner, that little brat. But did he listen? They never listen." His scent, a blend of onions, tomato sauce, and ripe armpits, washed over Parker like the breeze from a cheese factory. He nearly gagged.

Then his hackles rose. Glaring his best glare, Parker growled a primitive, saber-toothed-tiger sort of growl. But the man just chuckled.

"Snarl all you like, tough guy." Mr. Double-Wide sneered. "You're mine now."

And with that, he patted the top of the cage, stepped outside, and pressed a button. With an ominous whir and a click, the door slid shut.

*No. This can't be happening.*

Slowly, slowly, Parker sank onto the cold steel floor beneath him. His vision narrowed to a long black tunnel, and he could barely breathe.

A whimper escaped his throat.

No way around it. No way out.

This time, Parker was well and truly trapped.

⇦BOOF

# 18

# Playdate with a Punk

At first, the playdate was all Boof could've wished for. Rottweiler Boy greeted him at the door with a grin and a clap on the shoulder. Sure, the wallop felt kind of hard, but Deke probably didn't know his own strength.

Boof walloped him back. The big boy's eyes narrowed, but he forced a chuckle.

"Come in," said Deke. "You haven't been here since . . ."

"Ever," said Boof, while the other boy said, "Second grade."

"Sure," said Boof. He looked around with interest.

The house sprawled out in all directions like a Great Dane on ice, much larger and fancier than Boof's home. Some kind of shiny stone decorated the entryway floor, and a staircase broad enough to handle a team of horses led to the house's upper levels. Stealing glances into the rooms they passed, Boof noticed loads of deep, ivory-colored carpet; statues fashioned from some kind of white rock; and in one room, a picture box that covered almost an entire wall.

"Let's grab a snack, pal," said Deke, with another of those smiles that didn't reach his eyes. Boof was starting to think this was the boy's normal expression.

"I could eat," said Boof. Which was true. He was always hungry.

At a round table on one side of the kitchen, someone had set out a tall container of liquid and two glasses, plus two plates heaped with those treats humans called cookies. Boof began to sit down.

"Not there," said Rottweiler Boy, ushering him into the other chair. "Over here. These cookies were made special, just for you."

As Boof settled in, Deke poured them two glasses of the yellowy liquid, which had a sharp smell to it. Handing one glass to Boof, he clinked it with his own.

"Cheers."

"What are we cheering?" asked Boof.

"Uh, trouble to our enemies," said the big boy, taking a sip.

The liquid was so tart, it made Boof's mouth pucker. But in a good way. He slurped down some more.

Picking up a cookie from his own plate, Deke motioned

to Boof's treats. "Eat up," he said. "It's a, uh, old family recipe." His small blue eyes watched closely.

Never one to refuse a treat, Boof lifted a cookie to his mouth. Something about it smelled familiar. As he bit into the treat, Boof noticed Deke's lips and cheeks tightening, almost as if he were trying to suppress a smile. This boy must really love feeding people.

After a couple of bites, the flavor spread through Boof's mouth, and he recognized it at last. It was something he hadn't eaten much recently but had missed.

"Kibble," he said.

Deke burst out with a harsh "Haw, haw, haw! You ate dog food!"

"And not the cheap stuff either," said Boof, wolfing down the first cookie and picking up a second. "This is *good*."

The big boy's laugh cut short, as if he'd choked on a rawhide chew.

"You *like* it?" asked Deke.

"I love it."

The other boy's jaw fell open as Boof proceeded to eat the entire plateful, pausing only to sip some of the tart drink.

At last, Boof belched. "Now, *that's* a treat." He eyed Deke's cookies. "Are you going to eat yours?"

Deke's lips tightened. "You know what?" he said. "Let's go play a video game."

"What about Ball?" asked Boof, disappointed.

"Right after that." Deke led the way back down the gleaming halls and into the room with the enormous picture box on the wall. He gestured proudly. "This is the eighty-six-inch, ultra-HD model with surround sound. Check it out up close."

"Oh," said Boof. Rottweiler Boy might as well have been speaking Raccoon, but Boof went over and examined the picture box. When he turned around, he noticed Deke quickly edging away from a chair.

The big boy scooped up two black boomerang thingies—much larger and fancier than the ones at Gabi's house—and handed one to Boof. "Sit down." He motioned to a wide, tree-brown armchair.

As Boof sat, he felt something squish under him. A familiar odor teased his nostrils.

"Eeww, I smell something gross," said Deke, with a nasty smile. "Is it you?"

Boof sniffed. "I don't know." Rising from his chair, he bent low over the seat and took a deep whiff. "Ooh, nice and ripe."

Deke guffawed, pointing at Boof's rear. "You sat in poop! Eeeww, gross!"

Boof ran a finger through what remained on the chair and brought it up to his nose for closer inspection. This human nose lacked the scope and power of his former sniffer, but he could swear the brown smear was . . .

"Cat turds," said Boof.

"Parker pooped his pants, Parker pooped his pants!" chanted Deke in a taunting singsong.

It really was a powerful stink, with lots of robust character. Boof sniffed again. Such a shame to waste a good stench. Bending low, he rubbed his shoulder in what remained of the cat poop, enjoying it so much that he rolled over and made sure to get some on his back.

Deke's eyes popped and he sputtered, "You . . . but . . . you . . . you're sick," he said at last. "Are you crazy?"

Boof grinned up at him. "It disguises your scent. Try it. Might make you smell better."

In a flash, Deke's look of disgust flipped to a dark scowl. One meaty hand grabbed Boof's shirtfront and hauled him to his feet.

"I'm gonna clean your clock," he snarled.

"Is it dirty?" Boof frowned. "Everyone wants me to clean something."

"Freaky Dekey," said a snide voice from behind them. "What are you doing?"

"Ryker." Without releasing Boof's shirt, the big boy

turned. Suddenly, his tone sounded more tentative. "Teaching this punk a lesson?"

In the doorway stood an older boy, broader, taller, and stronger-looking than Deke, but with the same beady blue eyes. Boof wondered if the two were from the same litter.

Ryker sneered. "Aw, what'd he do, steal your lollipop?" He swaggered into the room like a Doberman who Boof had once met at the dog park.

"He, uh, bit me," said Deke, barely audible.

"*Bit* you?" Taking a quick step closer, the new boy cuffed Deke on the side of the head. "And you let him? What kind of wuss does that?"

Deke cowered as Ryker struck him again. "I—Ow! He surprised me."

"You're pathetic." With one muscular paw, Ryker pushed the smaller boy in the chest. Deke staggered back, falling into the chair. Realizing where he was, he quickly leaped up, brushing off his pants.

Boof raised a hand to Ryker in a little wave. "I'm Boo—uh, Parker."

"Who cares?" Picking up one of the boomerang thingies, Ryker flopped onto the couch. "Get lost, both of you. This is mine." He turned on the picture box with a small black stick.

"But—" Deke began.

"Beat it." The bigger boy's glare was hotter than a summer sidewalk.

Deke's lower lip trembled, but he masked it with a scowl. "Come on, Parker."

"Stinks in here," Ryker complained as they left the room.

Stomping through several more oversized rooms stuffed with furniture, Deke kept going until he shoved his way through a door into the backyard. Beyond a cluster of couches on the stone patio stretched a huge blue pool shaped like a giant bean. To either side, perfect green lawn rolled toward impeccably trimmed bushes. Random human toys lay abandoned on the stone patio. Some of them, Boof noticed, were balls.

"You wanna play?" snarled a red-faced Deke, scooping up a fist-sized white sphere. "Let's play." He pointed to the grass, and Boof jogged past him onto the lawn.

*This is going to be great*, he thought.

Just as Boof turned to glance back, the ball grazed his shoulder and ricocheted toward the bushes. "I wasn't ready." Retrieving it, he clumsily tossed the ball back to Deke. "Try again."

This time, Deke's face scrunched up until his eyes almost vanished. He twisted his body, cocked his arm, and fired hard, right at Boof's head.

Boof ducked, and it blew past. "Better," he said, chasing the ball and digging it out of a bush. He tossed it back. "Again."

By now, Deke's face had turned such a deep red it was almost purple. He gritted his jaw and hurled the ball even harder—this time, straight at Boof's chest.

Boof's human body was slow to respond, but he managed to raise his hands into catching position. *Bam!* The sphere slipped through and smacked him in the chest.

"Ow." Boof rubbed the sore spot. Rottweiler Boy really didn't know his own strength. Then he bent, scooped up the ball, and tossed it back. "Once more."

Deke ignored the sphere. He stared, arms hanging loosely. "What the flork is wrong with you?"

"Huh?"

"I feed you dog food, I put poop on your chair, I hit you with a ball, and you still want to *play*?" The boy sounded angry and confused, but Boof couldn't for the life of him figure out why. He was beginning to wonder if Deke didn't like him.

"Well, yeah," he said. "That's why I came over."

Deke's hands rose to his head and grasped two fistfuls of hair. A groan passed his lips. *"Why?"*

Boof shrugged. "You asked me. Plus, no one will play Ball with me."

That did it for Deke. Throwing his hands in the air, he gave a wild cry and ran straight at Boof.

Boof grinned. *Chase* was one of his favorite games.

He let Deke get close but not too close, and then he exploded into action. Around the pool, between the furniture, through the bushes, and back around the pool they ran, with Boof laughing all the way.

"Can't catch me!" he cried.

Deke just roared.

Sure enough, after a couple of minutes of this, Boof's prediction was proved true. Deke couldn't catch him. The bigger boy staggered behind, panting heavily.

"You . . . not supposed to . . . I can't," he gasped.

Boof turned to watch. Deke's face had gone the color of one of those round, mushy things Parker's mom had made him eat at dinner. He wore the wounded expression of a German shepherd pup when you take away his favorite chew toy.

"I . . . give up," Deke panted, keeling over sideways onto a poofy chair. "You're . . . no fun . . . to pick on anymore."

And just like that, the game was over. Boof cocked his head. He wanted everyone to like him, but it was dawning on him that not everyone was likable. He approached the chair, stopping just out of arm's reach. "Okay. I'm going home."

Stretching out a feeble hand, the big boy wheezed, "I don't . . . get it. You . . . so friendly . . ."

"Bye-bye," said Boof. "Your food is good, but you play too rough, and you smell funny."

Oddly, he didn't want to be friends with Rottweiler Boy after all. But he could think of someone else who would make a much better friend, if he took the time to say those magic words to him.

And with that, Boof turned away, passing through the huge, fancy house, out the tall, fancy door, and back down the streets to his home.

It was time to talk to his Boy.

PARKER⇨

# 19

# End of the Line

Built like a prison for animals, the county pound was all cold concrete and chain-link fences. Beneath the chemical smell of harsh disinfectant, it reeked of urine, poop, and a deep, pervading sense of fear. The whines, whimpers, barks, and yowls of dogs, cats, ferrets, and other unfortunates echoed off the walls until Parker could hardly hear himself think.

Despite Parker's best efforts to escape, Mr. Double-Wide had dragged him into a long, narrow kennel before releasing the snare and locking him in. Rough concrete chafed Parker's paws as he paced, up and down, up and down. He checked out his cell. The front corner sported a built-in water bowl. *Woo-hoo.* At the rear of the kennel, someone had spread straw and a threadbare blanket, presumably for his comfort.

Straw? Seriously? What was he, a cow?

Parker's heart thudded like AT-ATs in pitched battle.

His tail tucked between his legs and his head drooped in despair. Still, he tried to come up with a plan. He couldn't squeeze under the fence. Maybe Parker could lure over one of his jailers by barking his head off, and then . . . what?

If they carried a key ring, Parker might be able to slip his paw through the fence and touch it. But how would he grab it? And even if he could somehow drag the key into his cage, how would he turn it in the lock without a wrist, fingers, or opposable thumbs?

Parker whined in frustration.

He decided that if one of the workers took him for a walk, he would try to make a break for it. But the afternoon stretched on. No one came.

Parker needed to use the toilet. Of course, there was no toilet. Maybe that's what the straw was for? Skin crawling, he padded into the farthest corner of the kennel and did his business.

He didn't even want to walk on that floor, let alone lie down on it. Who knew how many dogs had messed there before him? After waffling about for a while, Parker picked a spot as close to the front of the kennel as possible and sat, tucking his tail around him.

"Hey, you," said a gruff voice. When Parker glanced up, he noticed the dog in the kennel across the corridor, watching him.

"Uh, hi," said Parker. He pushed his nose up against the chain-link and sniffed.

The other dog was smaller and older, some kind of Australian shepherd mix, and it was clear she'd seen some hard times. Her multicolored fur was matted, her right ear shredded, and one eye was missing. She looked gaunt and wiry, like the homeless guys Parker had seen panhandling downtown. She might have been living on the streets for a while.

"What are you in for?" asked the shepherd.

"Running wild, I guess," said Parker. "You?"

"Same." The other dog made a disgusted grunt. "They're threatened by our freedom."

Parker didn't know what to say to that. He'd always preferred his life to be nice and orderly, but he knew what the shepherd was talking about. Forget about dogs; grownups didn't even like *kids* to be too free.

"Did you run away?" asked Parker.

The dog fixed him with one fierce blue eye. "No, my owners did. They moved off one day, left me in an empty house."

A lump grew in Parker's throat. He knew how that felt, being abandoned.

"What about you?" asked the shepherd.

"Same." Parker swallowed. "Someone left me behind

too." In his mind's eye, he saw Mimi's smiling face. "It hurts."

"It does," said the other dog. Then, without another comment, she tilted her head back and gave a low howl.

It sounded so unbearably sad, so deeply lonesome, that Parker couldn't resist the despair any longer. His legs went wobbly, and he sank onto his belly. On and on the shepherd howled, like a coyote on the prairie, as the sun sank lower and night gathered.

At last, she fell silent. Both dogs were lost in their own thoughts. Soon, harsh fluorescent lights flickered on overhead, and footsteps slapped the concrete nearby. Mr. Double-Wide's distinctive odor arrived before he did, and Parker found his lips curling back from his fangs and a growl rumbling in his throat.

Whacking the chain-link with his snare, the dog-catcher sneered, "Zip it, mutt." Then he turned to the Australian shepherd. "Your time, princess."

As he opened her kennel door, the dog cringed in the corner, but there was nowhere to hide. In no time at all, the man looped his snare over her head and led her out.

"Are you getting a new family?" asked Parker.

She sent him a mournful one-eyed look. "No one came to see me."

"A walk, then?"

"They never walk us," said the other dog.

Parker frowned. "Then . . ."

"Who knows?" said the shepherd. "Maybe they're setting me free?"

"Maybe." But perhaps it wasn't the kind of freedom she was hoping for. Parker's body went heavy and cold. If she wasn't being adopted, and she wasn't going for a walk, there was really only one other option.

As the dogcatcher led her away, the shepherd twisted to look back at Parker. "Keep your tail up," she called to him. "Keep wagging. Maybe your humans will come." Then Mr. Double-Wide tugged her down the corridor, and in a handful of heartbeats, she was gone.

A high whine burst from Parker's throat. The unfairness of it almost broke his heart.

Some time later, who knew how long, one of the workers opened a slot in the fence and slid in a bowl of dry kibble. To Parker's sensitive nose, it smelled stale. He wasn't in the mood to eat, but his body demanded food, so he forced down a few mouthfuls.

Stale, and low quality besides. *Hey, look, I've become a dog-food connoisseur,* he thought. But his predicament weighed on his mind.

Parker was in grave danger. Even worse, nobody knew he was here. Shifting for comfort on the hard floor, he tried to picture the scene at home. None of them—neither Boof, his mom, nor his dad—would have any idea where he'd gone. They might drive around the neighborhood looking, but when they didn't find him, what then?

Would his parents think to check at the pound? Or would they tell Billie that her unruly dog had run off, and then go buy her a new dog—one that was much better behaved?

How long would Parker stay imprisoned here before the pound workers put him to sleep? Two days? Three?

The clock was ticking.

His stomach gave an uneasy roll. If he died at the pound, his parents wouldn't mourn him. They'd never even know. They believed their son was the same as he'd always been, if a little sloppier, and they thought of the dog as a discipline problem, not as the receptacle for Parker's soul.

Boof wouldn't mourn him. He'd slip into his role as Parker, raiding the fridge every day, making new friends, and misunderstanding almost everything that was said to him. Somehow he'd struggle through learning how to read and discovering the rules of human society. Parker felt almost sorry for Boof.

But he felt sorrier for himself.

His chin quivered. He'd lost his best friend, his grandma,

his body, his family. And now he just might lose his life. Parker's gut tightened.

As so many times before, he felt an irresistible urge to tidy up. Rising to his feet, he scouted around the narrow, sterile kennel for something to clean. The pee-stained straw? He shuddered. Never could he touch that again. All that remained was the built-in water dish, the food dish, and the ratty-looking towel.

Taking the towel gingerly in his teeth, Parker dragged it to the front of his cell, folded it in half, and arranged it as neatly as his doggie paws would allow. He repositioned the food bowl, then looked around again. Nothing else had magically materialized in the kennel, and all that restless energy still surged inside him, that burning need to restore order and sanity to the world.

But order and sanity were far, far beyond reach.

Out of options, out of hope, Parker flopped down on the towel and surrendered himself to black despair.

He longed for his dear Mimi with all his aching heart. She would've taken him in her arms and rocked him, as she had so many times, her sweet sandalwood smell making him feel like he was in the safest garden in the world. She would've talked things out and listened to Parker's fears. She would have made him see that things weren't as bad as he thought, that life was still beautiful, despite it all.

But Mimi was never coming back.

Ever.

For the first time, Parker let himself feel the whole awful truth of that, the sheer horror and finality of death. And then, he couldn't help it.

He wailed.

Even to his own ears, it was an unnatural sound, one that no dog had ever made, but Parker couldn't stop. He keened and keened until his throat was sore and he wore himself out.

And when at last he could wail no more, he slept.

⇦BOOF

# 20

# Ruby Lends a Paw

"Where's the dog?" asked Parker's dad shortly after he and Flower Woman came home. "Bird, have you seen him?"

Boof shrugged. "Not since I left to play at Deke's."

"Have you checked the backyard?" asked the woman. "Maybe he didn't hear us come in."

That, Boof knew, wasn't likely. Doggie Parker's super-sharp senses would've tipped him off for sure. In fact, now that Boof thought of it, where *was* Gloomy Boy? He'd searched the house and yard when he returned from his playdate, wanting to apologize for ignoring the warning about Deke. But when no Parker was found, Boof washed himself in the stand-up bath and tossed his shirt and pants in the dirty-clothes basket. (Strangely, the odor of cat poop wasn't as delightful as it used to be.) Then he took a nap to await Parker's return.

Which never came.

Ball Man opened the back door. "Here, boy!" he called. "Boo-oof!"

"What?" said Boof automatically.

Parker's father made a *be patient* gesture. "Nothing yet, son. Help me look for him."

*Parker, gone? This was bad. Very bad.*

Joining Mr. Pitts in the backyard, Boof yelled without thinking, "Parrrker!"

"Very funny."

*Oops.* Boof couldn't keep things straight anymore. He needed his Boy.

Parker's mom appeared at the back door. "He's not inside. Have you searched every corner of the yard? Maybe he's hurt."

Feeling kind of silly at calling his own name, Boof wandered about. "Boo-oof! Here, boy!"

With each minute that passed, Parker's parents grew more anxious. His Boy was missing. Boof felt his own heart sink, at their worry and his own.

Flower Woman produced a light stick, since night was falling and the last colors were fading from the sky. As they shouted for the dog, she splashed its beam around the edges of the yard, stopping when it illuminated a pile of fresh earth.

"Babes," she called to Ball Man. "Check it out."

All three converged in the back corner. At a glance, it was clear to Boof that Parker had dug his way into Ruby's yard—and done a pretty good job of it too, for a newbie dog.

"That's where he got out," said the Boy's father. "Come on, let's go next door."

*Why would Gloomy Boy want to escape?* wondered Boof as the three of them trooped out a side gate and through the yard to the neighbors' house. *This is his pack. He's got everything he needs here.*

It was a mystery, for sure.

A big, friendly-looking woman answered the door. "Why, it's the Pitts," she said. "A little early for trick-or-treating, aren't you?" She chuckled.

"Stephanie, have you seen our dog?" asked Parker's mother.

The woman shook her head. "No, but I heard him making some sad sounds yesterday."

"Looks like he dug under the fence and into your yard," said Ball Man. "Mind if we check?"

Swinging the front door open wide, Stephanie said, "Be my guest. He didn't come in with Ruby when I fed her, but maybe he's exploring our little jungle."

As they followed the woman through the house, Boof couldn't help noticing the enticing aroma of meat cooking with some kind of vegetables. His mouth watered.

"Smells good," he said.

"Why, thank you, dear," said Stephanie. "That meat loaf is my mama's recipe."

"Meat loaf," he repeated. Boof sure was learning a lot about the names of human food. He'd already learned spaghetti and eggplant and moo shu pork . . .

*Whoops. Focus, Boof.*

With an effort, he pulled his mind back onto the search for Parker.

The neighbor woman slid open her back door and flipped a switch, illuminating the bushy backyard. A couple of metal chairs showed amid the overgrown greenery, peering out like a sheepdog's eyes under shaggy brows.

"Boo-oof!" called the Boy's parents. "Here, Boof!"

They ventured deeper into the yard and split up, each taking a winding pathway. When one of the bushes suddenly came alive, Boof jumped back.

*Suffering cats!*

A massive, shaggy white dog emerged, planted her paws, and vigorously shook the leaves and twigs from her coat.

"Ruby?" said Boof.

"Gah!" It was the Great Pyrenees's turn to flinch. "How come ya speak Dog, human?"

"It's me, Boof. I'm in the Boy's body."

"Boof?" The colossal dog padded forward, sniffing curiously at Boof's pants legs and crotch. "Yeah, ya do smell kinda funny."

"Thanks," said Boof, who prided himself on his general stinkiness. He was bursting with impatience but politely sniffed Ruby's hind end in return. "Hey, can you help? It's important. We're looking for Parker."

"The one wearing your body?" asked Ruby. "That's some freaky stuff there."

"Tell me about it," said Boof, glancing down at his human form. "So, you seen him? Is he okay?"

Suddenly, one side of Ruby's mouth curled up in a snarl and her gaze turned savage.

"What's wrong?" asked Boof, uneasy. "Is it the Boy?"

"Flea!"

*"Flee?"* Boof crouched, ready to run.

Dropping back into a sitting position, Ruby scratched vigorously at her shoulder with a hind leg until she'd eliminated the pest.

"Ah, *flea*." Understanding washed through Boof. "Now, about the Boy?"

"You're not gonna like it." When Boof held out his hands in a *tell me* gesture, the big dog continued, "I followed him. Last I saw, he was being carried into the Bad Man's truck."

Boof frowned. "The Bad Man?"

Tossing her head impatiently, Ruby said, "Ya know who I mean. The guy who snatches dogs off the street."

All of a sudden, Boof's stomach felt fluttery, like he'd swallowed a mouthful of moths. He'd heard his family talking about Animal Control before, and about a place they called the pound. He remembered what they'd said.

"Not every dog he snatches comes back?"

"Not every dog he snatches comes back," Ruby confirmed.

They were silent for a few heartbeats, the Great Pyrenees sniffing a patch of grass, Boof turning over this new revelation in his mind.

If Parker didn't return, then Boof would be stuck in this body forever. He'd live a human life, eat human food, and grow up as a human.

Down a nearby path, Ball Man shone his light stick under bushes, searching for the missing dog. Flower Woman called out, asking if he'd found anything.

Boof scratched his jaw. What would happen if he just kept quiet and didn't tell Gloomy Boy's parents what Ruby had seen?

He would become the Boy.

All he had to do was keep his mouth shut, and he could raid that big cold box for food anytime he wanted. He could learn to understand those black marks on paper, take over the Boy's life, and . . .

Boof straightened up. He shook himself. This was human thinking. And though he might have lived inside the Boy's body for a few sleeps, he wasn't human.

He was Dog.

With dogs, pack loyalty was everything, and you didn't leave members of your pack behind. Ever.

There was only one choice for Boof to make . . .

"Hey, Dad!" He flagged down the Boy's father.

"Found something?" asked Ball Man.

Boof nodded. "Kind of. I think I know where he might be."

PARKER ⇨

# 21

# Countdown to Extinction

Nighttime in the pound was a lonesome thing. With full darkness, the animals' cries died down, but just when you started to drop off, some worried creature would yowl or bark you awake again.

Some of the wavering fluorescents stayed on, but they were as dim and distant as ancient lighthouses. The kennels pooled with shadows.

As a little kid, Parker had never been afraid of the dark. But this was different. Dread lurked in every shadow, the dread of the unknown. Parker didn't fear imaginary monsters, but his uncertain future had him plenty worried.

Who knew what would happen?

Sleep that night was fitful. When at last dawn smeared the sky and the fluorescents flickered off, Parker felt worn and bleary, like a scribbled note that's gone through the laundry in a jeans pocket.

He had no idea what time it was when he heard the first human sounds—a *shoof-shoof-shoof* coming down the corridor. Someone was sweeping up. A minute or so later, she rounded the corner, thrusting leaves before her with a wide push broom. The sturdy, dark-haired woman stopped at this cage or that, cooing some words of comfort here, scratching a cat through the fence there.

She had just reached Parker's kennel, when he heard footsteps smacking the cement from farther down the passageway. "Aw, you sweet guy," the worker said, extending her fingers through the cage for Parker to sniff. "I hope someone's coming for you soon."

Her hands smelled of tortillas and scrambled eggs, and her kindness made Parker's eyes prickle with unshed tears. He leaned against the chain-link so she could pet him, taking whatever comfort he could.

Warm and sure, the woman's hands found that spot behind the ears—the best place to scratch. Parker closed his eyes and gave himself over to the sensation.

"Don't waste your time on that one," said a high, tight voice. And Parker knew, even before opening his eyes, that Mr. Double-Wide was back.

"Aw, he's a sweetie," the woman said.

The man leaned a forearm on the chain-link and a whiff of sour armpit odor assaulted Parker's nose.

Seriously? This early in the morning? Had the guy never heard of deodorant?

"Don't get attached, that's all," said the dogcatcher.

"What do you mean?" asked the woman, straightening up and brushing her trouser legs.

"This one hassled me big-time." Mr. Double-Wide sneered at Parker. "I just put in his order. He's moving out."

The woman frowned, her dark brown eyes brimming with concern. "When did he come in, yesterday? That's not seventy-two hours."

"Don't worry your pretty little head about it." Extending an index finger, the dogcatcher *booped* her on the nose. "Now, get back to work, Sonya."

The woman stepped away, swiping at her nose with a forearm. "You first, *Donnie*." She glared as the thick man sent her a parting leer and waddled back down the corridor.

When he'd gone, Sonya dug a treat from her pocket, squatted down, and offered it to Parker. "I hope your people come for you soon," she said. "That guy is a stinker."

Although not a big fan of doggie treats, Parker took the morsel from her hand, so as not to hurt her feelings. But with Double-Wide Donnie's words ringing in his ears, he could barely choke it down.

This wasn't right. That lousy dogcatcher had had it in for him from the start. And now Parker was powerless to stop him. He whimpered.

"Aw, buddy." Sonya was still crouched down, watching him. "You look much too cared for to be a stray," she said, reaching into the cage and fumbling with his collar. "Do you have a tag?"

She turned his collar so she could read it. "Thought so." Casting a sharp glance after Double-Wide Donnie, she said, "I'm calling your family. That creep shouldn't break the rules."

Parker perked up. He licked her hand where it held his collar.

"You like that, eh?" Retrieving her cell phone from a pocket, Sonya squinted at the dog tag and dialed. It rang long enough to worry Parker. Finally, he heard the woman say, "Hi, it's Sonya Morales at the County Animal Control offices. Your dog, Boof, is here. Please call right away. It's urgent."

With one last scratch of Parker's head, she picked up her broom and went back to work. As she *shoof-shoof*ed away, Parker fretted. She'd left a message, which meant his parents were busy. He really hoped that Mom's cell phone number had been listed on his tag, because his dad sometimes forgot to turn his phone on at all.

How much time did Parker have left?

Would his parents arrive before the dogcatcher put him to sleep?

Unable to sit still, Parker paced the bounds of his cage, whimpering softly to himself. Could this really be his end? There was so much in life he hadn't done. He hadn't played on a school sports team, hadn't read the *Game of Thrones* books, hadn't visited Disney World—heck, he hadn't even talked to his crush, let alone kissed her.

It just wasn't fair.

The minutes ticked past and the sun slowly climbed. As time crept onward, Parker's heart burned like the Eye of Sauron and his mouth felt dryer than a week in the Gobi Desert. An agony of worry had him all wrung out.

And then, after what felt like half an Ice Age, a gate clattered and footsteps struck the cement. Pushed up against the chain-link, Parker strained to sniff.

Was it doom or salvation?

When his parents rounded the corner, he nearly fainted with relief. Boof and Double-Wide Donnie trailed behind them, the Animal Control officer griping about Parker all the way.

". . . Best not let him escape again," he was saying. "Your dog is a real handful—one of the worst I seen."

As they reached the cage, Boof pushed his way to the

front of the group, and when the man unlocked the door, he was the first one through it.

Parker rushed forward. Boof dropped to a knee, flinging his arms wide and hugging him.

"You're okay!" said Boof.

"*You're* okay," said Parker.

"I'm so sorry."

"I never thought I'd see you again." Parker leaned into Boof's embrace and reveled in the feel of warm hands in his fur.

His parents crowded around, petting Parker. His dad chuckled. "Bird, I never knew you were so attached to that dog."

"Are you kidding?" said Boof, looking Parker in the eye. "He's the best dog ever."

"The absolute best," echoed Parker, meeting his gaze.

⇧⇩

That night, when everyone had returned home again from school and work, the family ate dinner together, passing the dishes around and telling stories about their day. Parker sat patiently beside Boof's chair. For a change, Boof slipped him choice morsels every now and then, instead of hogging the whole plate for himself.

Later, after listening to Parker's dad play jazz piano and

watching some videos on the computer, Boof and Parker headed upstairs to get ready for bed. Boof still wasn't keen on the whole concept of tooth brushing, but he at least smeared some toothpaste around in his mouth, so Parker didn't push it.

At last they lay down to sleep, with Boof on the bed and Parker on the floor. Boof turned off the bedside lamp. Parker brought Mimi's statue down to comfort him. Wrapped around it, he lay there, listening to the faint sounds of the house: the creak of timbers settling, the TV downstairs, his parents' muffled voices. He breathed in the smells: dirty clothes, dust, the spring roll sauce from dinner.

Parker sighed. It felt so good to be home with his loved ones, no matter whose body he was in.

"Hey, Parker."

"Yeah, Boof?"

Dimly illuminated by moonlight, Boof rolled over to face him. "You were right about that big boy."

"Deke?"

"He wasn't a good friend. He tried to hurt me, and he played too hard."

"Told you."

Boof rose onto an elbow. "I know. I'll try to listen better."

Parker was quiet for a little while. He raised his head. "I'm sorry too."

"For what?" asked Boof, settling back down into the covers.

How to put it into words? Parker had to try. "You're right, I do need to loosen up more. Life is . . . messy. It's hard sometimes, and sometimes bad things happen."

"Good things too." Boof yawned. "Like the fridge. And playing Ball."

"That's true." Warmth slowly filled Parker's chest, and he felt a little misty-eyed. "Life is full of good and bad, all mushed together. And I can't control it. I can't change it. All I can do is just let it happen."

Boof said nothing.

"Know what I mean?" asked Parker.

But gentle snores told him that Boof had already fallen asleep.

## PARKER ⇨

# 22

# Birthday Boy

The next morning, the teasing scent of bacon and toast was the first thing Parker noticed. Eyes still closed, he breathed deeply, savoring the aroma. He yawned and stretched, and then he noticed something odd: blankets over his body.

Boof must have covered him up during the night. Cracking another titanic yawn, Parker opened his eyes, rolled over . . .

And found himself staring at his own nightstand, with the lamp, clock, and water glass in their usual places. Hardly daring to breathe, he lifted an arm and found himself gazing at a hand. A regular human hand!

Parker looked down, touching his chest and belly in disbelief. He gasped. A whoop escaped his lips.

*He was back.*

“I'm me!” he cried. “I'm me again!”

Kicking off the covers, Parker bounced out of bed.

Curled in a tight ball on the carpet, Boof raised his head.

"I'm back, buddy!" Squatting beside the dog, he ruffled Boof's fur. "*We're* back. What do you think of that?"

No answer. Boof gave a sleepy *wurf*, stretched up, and licked Parker's face.

The dog couldn't speak. The psychic link between them, or whatever it had been, was broken. Parker rocked back on his heels. Funny, he'd miss talking to Boof. But as the dog wagged his tail, Parker realized he could still understand him anyway.

And he was *back*.

"Come on, boy," he said. "Let's go get some breakfast!"

⇧⇩

Parker's birthday fell on the following Saturday. When his parents asked what he'd like to do, he requested a small party, just family and a few friends. He invited Cody and their mutual friend Raina. Just for Boof, he included the next-door neighbors and their dog, Ruby.

And wonder of wonders, he invited Gabriella Cortez.

When he'd returned to school as himself, Parker found that the ice had been broken with Gabi. She talked with him easily. She asked him to hang out with her and her friends at the mall. And even though she sometimes gave him a little side-eye, as if waiting for him to do something weird, Gabi seemed to enjoy his company as much as he did hers.

Even stranger, Deke no longer picked on Parker or demanded his lunch money. He was almost . . . *friendly.*

And all thanks to Boof. Of course, the dog had caused some troubles too. Parker discovered that Mrs. Scales had flunked him on a couple of quizzes, and Principal Anidi sent him a hard look whenever their paths crossed. But these things would resolve in time. (He hoped.)

Best of all, something had shifted in his feelings about Mimi. He still loved and missed her something fierce. A random memory of her could still bring a tear. But he felt more . . . accepting that she was gone. Now the joy of remembering her mixed together with the pain of her loss, somehow making the whole thing more bearable. It was bittersweet, like his favorite Chinese dish, sweet-and-sour chicken.

Of course, Parker still felt wary of Mimi's last gift, the wooden statue of Eshu. He left it on its shelf—better safe than sorry. But hey, catching a faint whiff of her perfume didn't send him into a tailspin anymore, so that was something.

On a warmish Saturday around two o'clock, Parker's guests began showing up. Cody and Raina came first, then Gabi and her redheaded friend, Jessica, followed by the neighbors. As Boof and Ruby rambled around the backyard, the rest of the guests played croquet and this goofy game of Cody's, where you held an empty ice-cream cone in your mouth and your partner tried tossing mini marshmallows into it.

Afterward, Parker couldn't stop himself from picking up all the marshmallows that had missed their target.

"There's our old Parker," said his mom with a wry smile. And it was kind of true, but it kind of wasn't at the same time.

"Let me help," said Gabi, grabbing a trash bag. And while Parker's dad cranked up the music, they squatted down on the patio and spent a companionable couple of minutes tidying up. When Gabi's shoulder accidentally brushed his, Parker swore he could feel a tingle where they touched. True, he often didn't know what to say to her, but she didn't seem to mind.

A favorite song came on, and the four adults whooped and began dancing in a painfully embarrassing way. Parker rolled his eyes at Cody. Gabi and Jessica shrugged. Raina said, "I hate when my parents do that" in sympathy.

They were all so distracted, they didn't notice Boof until he'd planted both forepaws on the picnic table and scarfed up most of the dip. Parker chased him off, but found that his irritation was mixed with amusement.

Boof was just being Boof. And it seemed like he'd kept some of his human taste preferences, just as Parker found the world of smells more alive than before.

When at last the ice cream cake emerged from the kitchen, Parker sat before it in the place of honor, carving slices for everyone. As he settled in to eat, he felt a nudge at his elbow. It was Boof. The dog's chin rested on the table, and his eyes kept cutting back and forth between Parker and the cake.

Parker laughed. Maybe the dog had learned a little something from his time as a human. "Well, since you're being so good . . ."

Into the kitchen he went, with Boof at his heels. Although he knew the dog would've happily scarfed up a slice of ice-cream cake, Parker dug out something more appropriate: leftover turkey from the night before. And he made sure to share some with his doggie mentor, Ruby.

After Parker had opened his presents and everyone had given him their best wishes, the party began to wind down.

Soon, only family remained. Parker started collecting the dirty plates and cups, but his dad shooed him away. "You're the birthday boy. Let your mother and me handle this."

At loose ends, Parker wandered across the yard to where

Boof lay in the last patch of light from a setting sun. He sat down beside the dog, and Boof thumped his tail in welcome. Idly, Parker watched his parents.

*What a week. If they only knew . . .*

Parker's hand found its way to that spot behind Boof's ears, and the dog leaned into his touch, savoring the sensation. Every time he faltered, Boof pushed against his hand again.

"Thanks, buddy," said Parker.

Boof gazed up at him with those amber eyes. Now that he'd spent a few days behind them, Parker had some idea what the dog was seeing.

A boy, far from perfect, but far from terrible. Someone who had loved and lost. But someone who could still love, still embrace life in all its messiness.

A corner of Parker's mouth tugged up in a smile. He sniffed the breeze, and it was ripe with possibilities.

There was a whole lot more life to be lived. Why not get started right away?

He looked down at Boof. "Does someone want a walk?"

The dog's wag answered as loudly as if he'd still been able to speak.

"Then let's go," said Parker. And off they went into the world together, light of heart and looking for adventure.

# Acknowledgments

You would think it'd be pretty simple to write a book about a boy and his dog, right? Nothing could be further from the truth. First, it took a surprising amount of research. I found particular help from Alexandra Horowitz's *Inside of a Dog: What Dogs See, Smell, and Know* and *The Other End of the Leash* by Patricia McConnell. Luckily, when I got in trouble with the writing, I had some terrific friends to help me. Thanks first to Joe "Jose" Sannazzaro, who helped me understand the OCD spectrum and the challenges faced by kids who lose a loved one. Thanks also to my true-blue agent, Steve Malk, for some helpful early guidance on the story, and my editor, Amanda Maciel, who kept saying "more Boof!" And finally, a major mahalo goes out to my beta readers, Lee Wardlaw and Gaby Triana. Many of the clever bits and much of the emotional resonance of the story are due to their insightful suggestions. Any mistakes are my own.

## About the Author

**Bruce Hale** is the Edgar-nominated author and/or illustrator of more than fifty seriously funny books for children, including the Chet Gecko, School for S.P.I.E.S., and Class Pets series. He lives in Southern California, where he is also an occasional actor, Latin jazz musician, and award-winning storyteller. You can find him online at brucehale.com.

# Meet the CLASS PETS

What do class pets get up to when students aren't around?
Adventure—and lots of trouble!